THREE
MOTHERS,
ONE
FATHER

Three Mothers, One Father

by

Sean Hogan

BLACK SHUCK
SHADOWS

Black Shuck Books
www.BlackShuckBooks.co.uk

First published in the UK by Black Shuck Books, 2020

978-1-913038-49-6

for Gary McMahon, who welcomed me in

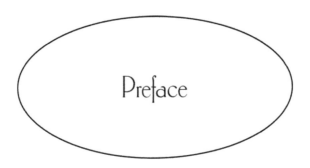

Preface

A very brief word of introduction – the work you are reading now is a semi-sequel to my previous book *England's Screaming*. If you are already familiar with that publication, I need say no more. If not, however, you may wonder what the hell this little book is all about. In which case, I must shamelessly point you towards the earlier volume and my foreword therein, in which I offer some explanation as to the influences and thinking behind this small indulgence (rapidly becoming an ongoing project) of mine.

Who's that yonder all in flames
Dragging behind him a sack of chains
Who's that yonder all in flames
Up jumped the Devil and he staked his claim on me

—'Up Jumped the Devil',
Nick Cave and The Bad Seeds

~

'All of them witches'

—Rosemary's Baby (1968)

Cast of Characters

The Devil

Marina Yaru in 'Toby Dammit', *Histoires extraordinaires* (Spirits of the Dead), 1968
written by Federico Fellini & Bernardino Zapponi
directed by Federico Fellini

Once the film had finished and the house lights had come up, the Producer slowly relit his cigar, chewed it furiously, then turned to the Director and told him, *Well, I can't sell this damn picture, and I sure can't eat it.*

The Director's habitually hangdog expression did not alter – it would be difficult for him to look any *more* depressed – but deep inside, he felt a part of his soul wither. This film was his crowning achievement, his masterpiece. After years spent labouring in low-budget genre movies, he had finally succeeded in putting something truly personal on celluloid, only to be told by this cigar-chewing peddler, this *hack*, that he couldn't sell it. As though it were nothing but a sack of spoiled potatoes.

The Producer continued. *Call this a Devil picture? I don't understand a goddamn word of it.*

Who are all these people moping around this old villa?
Are they alive or dead or what? And who's the bald guy
sucking a lollipop? Are you telling me that's meant to
be the Devil? You think Sam Arkoff is gonna buy this
arty-farty bullshit?

The Director closed his eyes and shrugged
hopelessly, saying nothing. Words were not,
after all, his thing. *Images* were, and this film
contained some of the most beautiful visual
arias he had ever conceived. It was a sumptuous
fever dream, a love letter to morbidity and
death. But it was no use sending such a missive
to a witless barbarian who lacked the sensitivity
and education to even read it in the first place.

When he reopened his eyes, he found himself
lost in a thick, gothic fog. Suddenly
disorientated, he felt as though he were trapped
in one of his earlier movies. *La maschera del
demonio* perhaps, or *Gli orrori del castello di
Norimberga*. The Director wanted to escape, to
flee the screening room, but had no idea which
way to turn. Such was the parlous state of his life
and career at this instant.

But moments later, the fog lifted. Of course,
it was only cigar smoke. He found himself
staring into the eager, gleaming eyes of the

Producer. The Director had learned to distrust that gleam. It usually meant the Producer had an idea, as hopelessly oxymoronic as that statement might be.

Listen. Have you seen The Exorcist? *Now, that's a Devil picture! Blood and blasphemy sure as hell put asses on seats! That movie has made more money than God. You gotta admit, Old Nick's onto something there!*

The Director was forced to admit he hadn't seen it. He'd heard of *The Exorcist* of course – everybody had by now – but he was still a fearful Catholic boy at heart, and the thought of watching a child say and do those terrible things, well, it just wasn't right. He'd always prided himself on taking even the most unpromising material and elevating it with his customary patina of cinematographic elegance, but where was the elegance in a young girl abusing herself with a crucifix?

The Producer was in full flow now. *You* gotta *see it. It could be just what our picture needs. A nice little exorcism! Imagine our heroine going to town on herself with a set of rosary beads! Listen, I'll book you on the next flight to London so you can catch a screening. Sound good?*

The Director sighed and got to his feet, the battle already lost. He was, after all, a gentleman, and therefore felt obliged to do whatever he could to help the Producer recoup his investment, even if it meant destroying his cherished dream. He nodded in weary assent, and turned to leave.

As he shuffled exhaustedly out of the screening room, he heard the Producer call after him.

Of course, I'll have to deduct the plane fare outta your fee. I'm on the hook for a lotta money here, and every dollar counts!

~

There's your daily bread! Eat it! Eat it like you did those whores' cunts before you became a priest!

His eye pressed to the camera viewfinder, the Director looked across at his actors; at the wooden American in priest's robes, dripping with fake vomit; at his lovely leading lady, her perfect face mutilated and scarred; and in that moment, he wanted nothing more than to throw up himself. The image of the room began to lurch and wobble, like a cheap special effect. Looking up from the viewfinder, he put his hand over his eyes, fighting back nausea.

Distantly, he heard the Producer call out: *Cut! Beautiful! Just beautiful!*

The Director was in such distress that he couldn't even summon the ego to be outraged at the Producer brazenly impinging on his directorial authority. How on earth could he call this depraved filth *beautiful*?

The man continued to bellow. *Know what I smell, people?*

The Actress's voice, lilting and soft. *Pea soup?*

A volley of uproarious laughter, sounding no less insincere for all the times it had been publicly practiced. *No, but it's green all the same! We're gonna make a lot of money here!*

We! The Director had to admire the Actress's restraint. She wasn't even being paid for these reshoots. He couldn't stay in this room, breathing this man's rancid fumes, a single second longer. Murmuring his apologies, he stumbled from the set, gasping for air.

The Producer followed swiftly at his heels, a bloodhound in pursuit. *What the hell's the matter with you?*

He *was* in a Hell, the Director decided. *I...cannot. I cannot do it.*

What are you talking about? We agreed!

It's blasphemy!

Of course it is! That's what the kids want these days! God is dead, haven't you heard?

Not my God.

The Producer chewed his cigar in rapid contemplation, proving he could at least think and masticate at the same time. Finally, he opened his arms wide in a gesture of expansive magnanimity. *OK, OK. Go ahead and take the rest of the day off. I'll fill in for you. What the hell, we only need to pop off a coupla singles, right?*

As though *that* was all there was to directing. Still, this was no time to debate the finer points of his craft. *Yes, yes, of course.*

But I want you back on set bright and early tomorrow, understand?

Si.

The Director hurried away before the Producer could change his mind, which was a frequent habit of his. That, and appropriating other people's good ideas as his own.

During the car ride back to his hotel, he could only think about how relieved he was to have left the Devil back on set. *Get thee behind me, Satan.* For that obscene, vomiting monstrosity was nothing he recognised as the Prince of

Darkness. *His* Devil was urbane, charming, louchely wicked. You didn't tempt people into wickedness by spewing into their lap, after all.

But having put one Devil safely behind him, the Director entered his hotel room to find another lying in wait. Of course, he did not initially recognise his visitor for what She was. What he saw at first was only an angelic little girl, dressed all in white and playfully bouncing a ball against the carpet.

It was only when She looked up and he saw the unmistakeably malefic expression on Her face that he knew.

The Director collapsed heavily into a chair. *Oddio! A little girl?*

The Devil playfully tossed him the ball. *Whenever it suits me. I always try to dress for the occasion.*

I must confess, I have never heard of such a thing.

Oh, I looked just like this when I tempted the Nazarene down from the cross. They usually leave that part out, though.

The Director crossed himself. *The Father of Lies,* he muttered.

The little girl shrugged. *Believe whatever you like. Can I please have my ball back?*

Still shaken by the bizarre turn of events, the Director threw Her the ball, but misjudged the strength of his throw and sent the ball crashing into a mirror hanging on the nearby wall. Shards of glass rained to the carpet.

The Devil shook Her head sadly, but the Director waved Her away. *My luck cannot get any worse.*

Well, I'm here to see what we can do about that.

What do you care about my luck?

The Devil came and knelt beside him. She looked up at the Director, Her pale face framed by blonde ringlets, and smiled. If anything, Her teeth were even whiter than Her dress, dazzling in their luminescent purity. She was a vision of Paradise.

The effect of the smile was to make the Director feel utterly, irredeemably damned.

Please understand, the Devil told him. *I'm a devoted fan of your work, maestro.*

The Director cackled in disbelief. *What does the Devil know of my work? I'm just a poor horror director. What about Antonioni, or Fellini?*

It is your name they will be murmuring reverently in fifty years time.

More lies!

The Devil tutted. *You should not believe everything you hear about me. I am a great patron of the arts. Cinema in particular.*

Then tell me your favourite actor.

Oh, that's easy. The great Toby Dammit.

The Director looked grave. *A sad loss to our profession.* The actor had died in a freak automobile accident just a few years earlier.

Indeed, the Devil replied. *I can't imagine whatever possessed him to try and jump that bridge.*

Her eyes twinkled, making the Director feel suddenly uneasy. The gleam he saw there put him uncomfortably in mind of his Producer. Now *there* was someone who could teach the Great Deceiver a thing or two about lying.

He leapt to his feet, suddenly animated. *All right, you've convinced me. Let no one doubt that the Devil is a true cineaste! But why are you here, now?*

Do you not think that I would know you were shooting a movie about me? the Devil said smugly.

Humbled, the Director seemed to visibly diminish in stature. His face crestfallen, he crossed to the window and stared out at the bustling streets of Rome. The city was going about its collective business, oblivious to the diabolic goings-on that were unfolding right under its nose.

It is not *about you,* he sighed, finally. *I already shot that picture. This...this is an abomination. It is unworthy of you.*

The Devil got to Her feet, retrieved Her ball, and began to bounce it against the wall. Its rhythmic thumps seemed, to the Director, to be counting down the seconds to his imminent damnation. *Yes, yes, I know all that.*

Are you here to punish me, then? For selling out? For painting you as a wretched, foul-mouthed thing?

Not at all, the Devil replied pleasantly. *I came to see if you wanted your movie put back the way it was. The way it* should *be.*

There was silence for a moment, then the Director turned from the window, barely able to believe such a thing might be possible. A plaintive tremor crept into his voice. *You could do this?*

Of course.

But why?

I already told you, maestro. I am simply a respectful admirer of your art. Not only that, but you have always endeavoured to portray me and my works fairly. La maschera del demonio, *what a movie!*

The Director nodded sadly. It seemed like such a long time ago.

The Devil daintily extended one small hand. *It's settled, then?*

So disarmed was the Director by the Devil's professed fandom, so eager was he to save his threatened magnum opus from destruction, that he barely considered what he was about to do. *That's it? We just shake hands? Don't I have to sign a contract or anything?*

The Devil rolled Her eyes. *I'm not after your immortal soul, maestro. Think of this as a small favour. I'm happy to be able to give something back for all the many hours of pleasure you have brought me.*

The Director seized her hand and shook it eagerly. *Then yes! Yes!*

Months later, when the bastardised version of the film he had cherished so much was released and became his biggest box-office success to date, the Director was left to reflect upon the dubious wisdom of making deals with the Devil.

For it was not that his diabolic visitor had lied, exactly – people would indeed get to see the version of the picture that the Director had originally intended – but that, as was always Her way, She had neglected to mention certain pertinent details.

Such as the fact that, forever dogged by his perpetual bad luck, the Director would meet a somewhat premature end in 1980, aged only sixty-five, while his doomed, morbidly romantic masterpiece would not be publicly seen in its intended form until 1983.

Bruno Legnani

Toninio Corazzari in *La casa dalle finestre che ridono*
(The House with Laughing Windows), 1976
written by Pupi Avati & Antonio Avati
directed by Pupi Avati

No one who has seen a work by Bruno Legnani can honestly profess themselves unmoved by the experience. The level of suffering and violence that permeates his art is such that one wonders how any canvas could be sturdy enough to withstand it; every brushstroke feels like a knife wound, slowly bleeding the spectator white. *My colours are soft like blood, smooth like syphilis*, he was fond of saying. Small wonder, then, that galleries exhibiting his work have reported patrons passing out, being taken ill, or in some cases even collapsing in fits, upon viewing the paintings.

The Painter of Agonies, they called him – at least, the few who were even aware of his name. Little-known in his own time – unsurprising given the uncompromising morbidity of his work – Legnani never left the small town in

Northern Italy he was born in, and committed suicide in 1931 by setting himself on fire. But over time, as the myriad horrors of the 20th Century took hold, the *zeitgeist* caught up with Legnani's art, and his reputation began to build.

And along with it, the rumours. Appalled whispers that such visceral imagery could not possibly be entirely imaginary, and that actual violence – even murder – had been committed in its pursuit. Still, nothing was ever proven; the painter was no longer around to answer to the truth of the assertions, and his only surviving family, the two sisters who had shared his home (the locally-notorious 'House with Laughing Windows', the sobriquet derived from the discomforting grins Legnani had painted around each window frame) and supported him in his work, had long since vanished.

Whatever the truth of the matter, there can be little doubt that the gossip only made Legnani's work even more desirable in certain, more decadent quarters. The notorious Satanist Hjalmar Poelzig was an early devotee of the painter, although tragically, none of his small collection survived the explosion that destroyed his house and took Poelzig's life in 1934. In the late 1960's, the Farnsworth Gallery in Florida mounted the first public exhibition of Legnani's artwork in the US, prompting outraged local residents to picket the establishment. It is also said that reclusive industrialist Damien Thorn has a room in his country manor solely dedicated to the Painter of Agonies.

But for all of his posthumous fame and notoriety, and the attendant exhibitions and volumes of scholarly analysis dedicated to his art, there are three paintings by Legnani that have never been publicly displayed or discussed; indeed, their very existence is a closely-guarded secret, and almost completely unknown to the world at large. In the unlikely event they were ever put up for auction, they would doubtless inspire a bidding frenzy amongst wealthy collectors. Regardless, it is hard to imagine the circumstances under which such an occurrence might take place. Privately commissioned portraits, the paintings have never once left the houses of the three women who sat for them: Mater Suspiriorum, Mater Tenebrarum, and Mater Lachrymarum.

The Three Mothers.

Bruno Legnani had little interest in the

spiritual or esoteric, beyond the deranged Catholic-inspired fantasies that fuelled so much of his artistic output, but his two mysterious sisters were another matter. While their brother's solipsistic thirst for blood and pain was channelled solely into his art, their own madness led them to not only torture and kill on Bruno's behalf, but also to seek out other, even more terrible patrons. The sisters always understood that their brother's insanity could only ever end in his own death; his art was a terminal sickness that would inevitably consume him. They foresaw a time in which they would no longer be able to sate their own bloodlust in the service of Bruno's work, but the thought of spilling blood merely for its own sake seemed to them to be entirely frivolous, almost sacrilegiously so. What their brother called the *brutal nobility* of death was a transcendent, reverential matter to the sisters. Such holy tasks must only be performed in devotion to a higher power, whether that be Bruno Legnani's dark muse, or the three dread witches that made their home in the deepest, coldest shadows of the world; three women, sisters and mothers both, that held sway over the world, and who were far more viciously demanding and capricious than any muse.

So it was that the Legnani sisters entered the congregation of the Three Mothers. Following a gossamer trail of whispers and legends, they made a pilgrimage to Rome, eventually arriving at the damned house of Mater Lachrymarum. Taking along a small boy they had snatched from the city streets, they were eventually admitted to the great building's inner sanctum, where the Mother of Tears sat waiting for them, stroking a white cat that lay purring in her lap. Her beauty was legendary; the Legnani sisters had heard tales of men preferring to cut out their own tongues rather than risk saying anything vulgar or stupid to her and thereby diminishing themselves in her eyes. In this aspect, the visitors were not disappointed; so startling was Mater Lachrymarum's loveliness that even their young captive ceased his screaming at the sight of her.

Laura, the older of the two sisters, stepped forward. *Our gift to you*, she said, pushing the boy to his knees. *We offer you this child, and our devotion.* She then took out a straight razor and slit the child's throat.

The Mother of Tears looked bored. Her cat jumped down from her arms and began to lap at the scarlet tide spreading darkly across the marble floor. *What use have I for a dead child?* she said. *This world entire belongs to my sisters and I, and children die in their thousands across it every day.*

Then what shall we offer you? Laura pleaded. *We wish only to please you, and to serve.*

Their new mistress thought for a moment, an icy blizzard raging in her flawless blue eyes. Then she smiled. *There is something*, she said. *A service only you can procure.*

The sisters travelled back to their hometown. Upon arriving home, they climbed the stairs to the attic, where their brother kept his painting studio. They found him in the thrall of an opium daze, burbling lunacies into a recorder. A gutted corpse hung from a hook nearby, its entrails dangling down like shiny ribbons.

Brother, the sisters told him. *We have a commission for you. Three subjects, three portraits. The clients insist that only the Painter of Agonies can capture their true likenesses on canvas. They will pay any price.*

Bruno scoffed. *I do not paint portraits for the moneyed bourgeoisie!* he exclaimed. *The soft rosy pink of pampered flesh is not part of my palette. Only the thick crimson of man's lifeblood and the awful yellow of decay!*

Hush now, the sisters said. *Rest assured, you will find these subjects to your liking. They are darker and more terrible than even your vilest fantasy. And besides, brother, you have absolutely no choice in the matter.*

Over the course of the next several months, the Three Mothers each called on Bruno Legnani in turn, and sat for their respective portraits. It was a rare honour for anyone to be visited in their own home by the Mothers, let alone a man, and the Legnani sisters did their best to impress this fact upon Bruno, whose steadily-growing mania made his behaviour unpredictable at best. Still, the painter recognised unmitigated corruption when he saw it, and offered a once in a lifetime opportunity with such rare subjects, he managed to produce three canvases that ranked amongst his very best work.

~

Mater Suspiriorum

Painting the Mother of Sighs posed an interesting challenge. In recent times she had preferred to remain invisible to human eyes, and when she finally revealed herself to Legnani, he immediately understood why. Her sunken, sagging flesh was not only ravaged with the depredations of age, but worse yet, she appeared almost to be rotting from the inside out, as though the utter vileness at the core of her being had infected her very blood and tissue.

Of course, Legnani was delighted. *The colours, oh, the sweet colours,* he murmured.

The finished portrait is reminiscent of the work of Francis Bacon; *Figure with Meat,* perhaps, or *Three Studies for a Portrait of George Dyer.* In order to capture the rainbow of putrefaction that marked Mater Suspiriorum's flesh, Legnani resorted to exhuming several decomposing corpses from his own garden; previous subjects that had already served their purpose and been laid to rest by his ever-diligent sisters. Cultivating the bodies for the reeking fluids and juices of their dissolution, he mixed the effluents with his paints to create a palpable sense of rot, a portrait that almost seems to wither and decay before the viewer's very eyes. For the mad swirl of reds and browns that surrounded the central figure, Legnani utilised the functions of his own body, taking his blood and excrement and frenziedly daubing them onto the canvas with his fingers.

When he had at last completed the painting, Legnani found himself seized by a sudden terror. Like the undoubted artist that he was, he had striven to portray the unflinching truth about his subject, but what if the Mother of Sighs pronounced herself displeased with the results? What if her ageless vanity was so great and so terrible that when she saw the utter hideousness of the portrait, she flew into an insulted rage? What might arousing the anger of such a powerful and malign creature mean for a mere painter?

The artist needn't have worried. When she set her rheumy, yellowed eyes upon the finished work, Mater Suspiriorum inspected it with astonishment, leaned in to peer closely at the canvas, then broke into a fit of gleeful cackling. *Oh, you see a great deal, painter! Perhaps more than human eyes were ever meant to see! Mind what happens to you when you turn that gaze upon my sisters!*

~

Mater Tenebrarum

As her name suggested, the Mother of Darkness was a being of the shadows, and would only consent to sit for Legnani at night. Appearing to him after cockcrow, the Mother would arrange herself in the blackest corner of the attic studio, and forbade the painter to work by anything more than the dim light of a single candle. For an artist so devoted to his vivid colours, it was as though Legnani had been forced to paint without the use of his right arm. Still, he stoically accepted the rigours of the challenge, and laboured to create a portrait that is quite unlike anything else he ever produced.

To look upon the painting is almost to gaze into a void, an infinite space. It is a dizzying, uncomfortable sensation. The spectator feels as though they might stumble and plunge headlong through the canvas into bottomless darkness at any moment.

But, once the onlooker has managed to accustom themselves to the vertiginous experience of standing before the portrait, a curious thing happens; some form of bizarre optical illusion, perhaps. The figure of Mater

Tenebrarum seems to step forward from the shadows, gradually revealing herself from within the shroud of darkness that has hitherto concealed her. Quite how Legnani managed to create such a *trompe l'oeil* is a mystery. Although only the faintest outlines of the Mother's features are visible, the painter still managed to capture a tangible feeling of cruelty, suggesting absolute malignity with the merest of brushstrokes.

Not only that, but as one stares at the image, an uneasy feeling intensifies; an impression of unseen forces lurking behind Mater Tenebrarum, concealed in that empty nothingness and poised to strike at her command. The effect is to instil a feeling of complete dread and insignificance in the onlooker, a transfixed awe at the sheer level of malevolent power the subject wields.

It is no exaggeration to state that viewing the portrait is, in all respects, a terrifying experience.

Perhaps that is why Legnani insisted upon taking a restorative break after completing the painting. Always prone to the vicissitudes of his deranged temperament, he shut himself away in his studio for more than a week, refusing to eat or speak to his two siblings. For days he could be heard giggling and gibbering incoherently to himself, interspersed with manic episodes of ranting and howling. The sisters were quite accustomed to their brother's moods and rages, but nevertheless found themselves unusually alarmed at this latest episode. It was true that they feared what this strange commission might be doing to Bruno's already frayed sanity, but they dreaded the inevitable consequences should his mind snap completely before the work was finished even more.

~

Mater Lachrymarum

And then, one morning, Laura Legnani ascended the stairs to the attic bearing a bowl of fruit, hoping to persuade her brother to take some nourishment, and found the studio door open and unlocked. Inside, Bruno appeared docile, even cheerful, busying himself with the preparations for his next painting.

Sitting with him, stroking her ever-present feline companion, was the preternaturally beautiful young woman Laura remembered so vividly from the sisters' pilgrimage to Rome – the Mother of Tears.

Laura apologised for the interruption, made sure that their guest wanted for nothing, and excused herself. Downstairs, she remarked to her sister upon the drastic and sudden change to their brother's equilibrium. Such, it appeared, was the entrancing effect of Mater Lachrymarum's presence.

Bruno Legnani had always professed himself disinterested in beauty for its own sake. *The world is not beautiful*, he insisted, *so why must art be?* However, when it came to painting the Mother of Tears, it appears he purposefully discarded his own most fervently-held beliefs. As long and as hard as he had worked on the previous two portraits, he redoubled his efforts when it came to capturing the uncanny allure of the loveliest of the Three Mothers. For weeks he struggled, destroying dozens of failed studies and false starts along the way. On more than one occasion he was reduced to tears of frustration at the perceived limitations of his own talent (an occurrence which, one imagines, did not altogether displease his subject). In order to accurately portray Mater Lachrymarum, Bruno Legnani ultimately had to rebuild his entire methodology from scratch; to teach himself to appreciate absolute beauty.

During these long, abortive sessions, never once did the Mother of Tears utter a single complaint. She sat patiently and quietly, softly murmuring to her familiar and silently relishing the artist's suffering. It was obvious to all that Legnani had fallen obsessively in love with his subject, and knowing that he could never possess her, perhaps sought to protract the sitting for as long as possible. For the duration of their time together, artist and subject existed in a symbiotic relationship of exquisite pain, but such limitless agony can only be borne for so long.

The final portrait differs from the others in both methodology and content. The painting is a full-body nude, portraying Mater Lachrymarum reclining upon a turquoise *chaise-longue*. Her unknowable allure is evident and skillfully rendered by the artist; in contrast to his usual assaultive style, here Legnani's brushstrokes seem almost to caress the delicate swells and contours of his subject's anatomy, like a lover's gentle fingertips.

It was as close as he would ever get to touching her.

And yet, for all that, it is still possible to discern a trace of the familiar Legnani style in the portrait. Perhaps he was too infatuated with death to ever truly portray life – or perhaps it was simply the truth as he perceived it. Because, for all of her undoubted beauty, there is still an intimation of the grave in Legnani's rendition of the Mother of Tears. A sense that, concealed underneath the veneer of tantalising perfection, there lies a worm-ridden morass of gelid decay.

To put it bluntly: to look upon the portrait is to be seized by an irrepressible desire to fuck the subject, but in the certain knowledge that doing so would be a heedless act of wanton necrophilia.

There is one final tiny detail worth noting in Legnani's portrayal of the Mother of Tears. I have remarked before upon the glacial quality of her fathomless blue eyes, an aspect that the painter captures accurately and faithfully, but yet – if one examines the painting closely enough – it is possible to discern a small spark of incandescence within their cold depths. The faintest impression of a dancing flame, perhaps, lending a trace of warm amusement to the Mother's chill gaze.

I mention this only because it seems to be a fitting portent of what was to come.

Upon finishing the portrait, Legnani stripped off his clothes, then prostrated himself before Mater Lachrymarum, frenziedly masturbating himself to a climax. When he finally looked up, his dripping hands outstretched in supplication, the Mother of Tears had disappeared. Laura Legnani discovered her brother some hours later, still slumped naked on the studio floor, weeping uncontrollably.

The next day, he poured a can of petrol over himself, then calmly lit a match.

Before they had even finalised Bruno Legnani's funeral arrangements, his two sisters saw to it that his last completed works were delivered to the Three Mothers' respective houses in Freiburg, Rome and New York, where they were put on display in each of the buildings' cellars.

It is not known whether the Mothers offered any condolences over Bruno Legnani's death in return.

Trelkovsky

Roman Polanski in *Le locataire*
(The Tenant), 1976
written by Gerard Brach & Roman Polanski
based on the novel by Roland Topor
directed by Roman Polanski

Ever since his miraculous escape at age six from the liquidation of the Kraków Ghetto, Trelkovsky had considered himself a marked man. *I was meant to die along with my parents*, he would say. *But you'll see. One day, they'll get me.*

Quite who he thought *they* were, long decades after the war had ended, was open to question. If pressed on the matter, Trelkovsky would mutter darkly and light another Marlboro, his tobacco-stained fingers trembling as he lifted the cigarette to his lips. *What does it matter who they are? I'm a Jew, we were put here to suffer.*

And it was true, Trelkovsky did seem to possess a curious knack for calling down trouble upon himself. Despite his diffident nature, if a fight broke out in a bar where Trelkovsky was drinking, he would be certain to blunder unknowingly into the middle of the fracas, get blamed for causing it, and end up being thrown out onto the street as a result, while doubtless receiving a number of unprovoked punches along the way. The few friendships he attempted to nurture never lasted for long, as acquaintances would either hold him somehow responsible for matters that had gone wrong in their own lives, or else they would simply fleece the timid little man for all he was worth, until they finally grew bored of such easy sport and turned their attentions elsewhere. As for romantic assignations, on the rare occasions Trelkovsky managed to coax a woman into his bed, she would inevitably turn out to be unfaithful, unstable, or worse.

So when he lucked into finding a vacant Paris apartment, the previous occupant having recently attempted suicide, he was quite certain it was too good to be true. Some might have considered renting rooms which the last tenant had vacated by defenestrating themselves to be tempting fate, but not Trelkovsky, who had already resigned himself to the fact of his own inevitable, inescapable doom.

Still, things went smoothly enough at first.

True, the apartment was dingy and lacked its own toilet, but it offered more than enough space for such a small, unprepossessing man, and a stout front door capable of holding firm against the intrusions of the outside world. In a bid to pay his karmic debt, Trelkovsky even went as far as to visit the previous tenant – one Simone Choule – in hospital, where she lay shattered and comatose after her fall. Admittedly, she had suddenly awoken and screamed horribly at the sight of her unexpected visitor, but Trelkovsky was used to people reacting badly around him, and besides, he had even managed to pick up a grieving girlfriend of Simone's while at her bedside. Her name was Stella, and later that day, as they sat together in a darkened cinema, Trelkovsky's eager hand stroking her thigh, he told himself things were definitely on the up.

After a lifetime of ill fortune, Trelkovsky's optimism was touching, but sadly misplaced. Before much longer, his landlord and the building's other occupants began to turn against him, accusing him (unjustly, of course) of making too much noise. Not only that, but he discovered a human tooth nestled inside a small hole in the living room wall. Convinced it must have belonged to Mme. Choule, Trelkovsky began to be assailed by the creeping sensation that the woman was still with him in the apartment, her lurking influence growing steadily and surely, like putrid black mould upon the walls. He tried to tell himself that this was a ridiculous notion, but when laying in bed at night, he began to hear a soft voice murmuring inside his skull, as though the apartment's previous occupant had simply crawled inside his head and taken up residence there instead.

At such times, he would flee his rooms and take refuge in the floor's communal toilet, situated on the opposite side of the building. There, he would huddle in the darkness until the insinuating voice in his mind finally started to subside. As he sat huddled on the toilet seat, trying to avoid looking back through the lavatory window at his own apartment (best not to discuss the shadowy figures he frequently glimpsed lurking there, oh no), his furtive eyes would instead scan the cubicle walls, reading the years' worth of graffiti that had accumulated there.

There were the usual childish rhymes and

obscenities, but scrawled high in one corner, Trelkovsky found something else; three eerily evocative words he took to be Latin. He did not understand the language, but found that they somehow spoke to him all the same.

Suspiriorum.

Tenebrarum.

Lachrymarum.

Spoken together, the three names seemed to form a strangely disquieting litany. When he finally returned to his apartment, he fell asleep murmuring them.

The next day Trelkovsky hurried to the Bibliothèque nationale de France and began to research his discovery. He began with Latin dictionaries, which eventually led him to Thomas De Quincey's essay *Suspiria De Profundis*, which in turn took him to an obscure treatise written by an Italian alchemist named Varelli: *The Three Mothers.*

Within its pages, Trelkovsky read of the three women whose names he had discovered scratched in his lavatory wall; of how each of the Mothers dwelled in a terrible, damned house, and from there held sway over the world, their power and influence extending across the globe.

It was as if they were three venomous black spiders, squatting at the centre of a vast, inescapable web.

And was he, Trelkovsky, nothing but a helpless fly? Always quick to see a conspiracy lurking around every corner, he possessed little doubt that discovering their names had been no coincidence. Whatever had happened to Mme. Choule and was now happening to him was somehow connected to the Three Mothers, he was sure of it. Had *she* written those dread words upon the toilet wall? Trelkovsky longed to ask her, but the woman had died in hospital not long after his visit.

It was true; had the little man only been able to speak to his predecessor, he might indeed have learned some pertinent pieces of information. Such as the fact that Mme. Choule had originally trained as a ballet dancer at the renowned Tanz Akademie in Freiburg, Germany, a location that held malign significance for anyone versed in the dark history of the Three Mothers. And although her dancing career had been cut prematurely short by injury, the education Simone Choule had received at the Academy went far beyond mere ballet. In particular, the forbidden rituals she had learned at the feet of the academy's director, Helena Markos.

Or, as she was otherwise known: Mater Suspiriorum, the Mother of Sighs.

But of this, Trelkovsky knew nothing, nor would he ever. Such esoteric knowledge was denied to men like him; only a very few members of his despised gender would ever be permitted to learn but a fraction of the Mothers' secrets. The arcane wisdom Mme. Choule had brought back with her to Paris was hers and hers alone. Trelkovsky would, in one dreadful sense, ultimately be a recipient of it, but hardly a beneficiary.

He could not know, for instance, that the Three Mothers had mastered the art of transferring their essence into other bodies whenever it suited them; an insidious skill they occasionally taught to their acolytes. To master this ability was considered something of a rite of passage; for mortal beings, the rite was fraught with difficulty and peril, and only the most adept of the Mothers' children ever dared attempt it.

Simone Choule counted herself amongst their number.

In order to facilitate the process, Mme. Choule had first been required to place a piece of herself within her apartment's walls, then injure herself to the point of near death in order to loosen her soul's ties to her body. Had she been killed outright, the spell would have failed. But during the time that she lay in hospital, hovering between life and death, poor Trelkovsky had blundered unknowingly into her trap, and now the ritual could be completed. It was simply a matter of time.

Over the course of the days that followed, Trelkovsky's already-fragile grasp on existence began to be completely wiped away. It was as though his entire personality was merely a flimsy facade; a thin veneer of imagery that had been inexpertly applied over an existing oil painting, but which could now be stripped away to reveal the true portrait underneath. He soon began to don a wig and make-up, even dress in Mme. Choule's clothes; worse yet, people began to address him as though he *were* the dead woman.

Perhaps he was. Perhaps he always had been.

He suspected the rest of the apartment block of conspiring in whatever was happening to him, and when Stella tried to come to his aid, his crazed paranoia was such that he rejected her too. His sanity was a tiny, shrinking island, and in the increasingly rare moments of coherence he had left to him, he could only sit and watch the rising tide eat away at whatever was left of it.

Eventually, his mind simply collapsed under the strain. Now almost completely under Mme. Choule's influence, Trelkovsky attempted a final insane act of emulation and threw himself out of the apartment window. True to form, he survived – his lifetime of suffering could not be ended that easily – and so, with a lunatic display of will, he managed to drag his broken, bloodied carcass up several flights of stairs and do it again.

Now, the circle was complete.

The next thing Trelkovsky knew, he was lying in a hospital bed, unable to move. His limbs were full of shattered glass, his nerve endings vibrating with an endless symphony of agony. And yet, through all the pain, he was cognizant of one thing above all else – this ruined shell was not *his* body.

The undeniable truth of this seeming impossibility was revealed when he opened his eyes to see *himself* standing at the bedside, a distraught Stella clutching at his arm. Trelkovsky as he had been, all those long days before; guileless, forever eager to please. Flushed with the foolish conviction that his luck had finally changed.

And yet...

There was something else. Trelkovsky stared up into his own eyes and saw something alien. Someone else lurking behind the timorous gaze. Someone sly, and victorious.

He realised who it was, and screamed.

But even the paltry relief of releasing his own pent-up terror was denied him. For the sound that emerged was a high-pitched, womanly shriek.

When Mme. Choule left Trelkovsky's bedside, she immediately took a cab to Paris Gare de l'Est, then boarded the next train to Germany. Locking herself inside the toilet, she studied her new features in the mirror, and was not entirely displeased. True, Trelkovsky's frame was small, but nevertheless lithe and wiry.

An assassin's body.

When the train arrived in Karlsruhe, Mme. Choule disembarked and caught a connection to

Freiburg. By the time she arrived it was night, and a storm was raging overhead. Taking a cab to the Tanz Akademie, she was greeted at the door by a familiar face: the school's head instructor, Miss Tanner, who embraced her warmly.

My darling Simone, Miss Tanner told her. *Welcome back. I hope you're happy with how everything went?*

Mme. Choule nodded. *It's a bit like wearing new shoes,* she replied. *Uncomfortable at first, but everything adjusts to fit in time.*

Miss Tanner took her arm. *The headmistress is waiting for you.*

They proceeded through the corridors of the Academy to the Iris Room, where Tanner activated the secret door leading to the building's inner sanctum. The instructor then ushered Mme. Choule into a darkened chamber.

Inside, the air was filled with sighs. The room appeared empty, save for a small wooden chest sitting on a table.

Mme. Choule could sense Mater Suspiriorum nearby, invisible to the eye. Her desiccated croak sounded from the darkness, like a thousand tiny bones crackling underfoot.

You have done well, Choule.

Thank you, Mother.

There is but one final task to complete.

Mme. Choule opened the chest. Inside, nestled against a bed of crushed blood-red velvet, were three objects: a knife, a length of rope, and a pair of black leather gloves.

Her name is Patricia Hingle. She must not leave Freiburg alive.

Mme. Choule carefully removed the gloves from the box and slid them onto the still-unfamiliar set of male hands that now belonged solely to her.

A perfect fit.

Lucas Medev

Michaël Cohen in *Ils*
(Them), 2006
written & directed by
David Moreau & Xavier Palud

As he lay crippled and helpless in the sewer tunnel that would soon prove to be his tomb, Lucas Medev found his mind turning to beginnings, and endings. He thought back to his early life on the Spanish island of Almanzora, and to that terrible day when his childhood ended forever.

After all this time, her face was still etched indelibly in his memory. A blonde angel, appearing out of the unyielding sunlight, as radiant as if she were the sun's rays made flesh.

He had been idly playing in the dirt, poking at an ant's nest with a stick, when he became aware of a presence behind him. He looked around, shielding his eyes against the sun's glare – and there she was, a rubber ball cradled in her arms, smiling down at him. Lucas was sure he'd never seen her around the island before, and he thought he knew all the local children.

He was only six years old at the time and still far too immature to appreciate beauty – but nevertheless, he understood implicitly that the girl who stood before him was incandescent in her loveliness and purity. He knew immediately that he would do anything for her.

What's your name? she asked.

I'm Lucas. What's yours?

She giggled. *You can call me Lourdes.*

I haven't seen you before, Lucas said.

I'm new here. Do you want to play?

He did. *We can play with your ball if you want. Or you can help me kill these ants?*

Her face immediately twisted in displeasure. Lucas was shocked at how quickly her features could shift from beauty to ugliness, almost as if a veil had been ripped away from her face. *That's baby stuff. Anyone can kill stupid ants.*

Lucas found he very much did not want to be thought of as a baby by his new friend. *You think of a game then,* he told her shyly.

Lourdes smiled again, and Lucas immediately relaxed, basking in her renewed happiness. *I know a game, the best game*, she said with mounting excitement.

Her eyes quickly surveyed their surroundings. Nearby, a man lay slumped underneath a small grove of trees, dozing in the feeble shade cast by their withered branches. A bottle of cheap red wine was cradled in the crook of his arm.

Who's that? Lourdes asked.

That's Francisco, Lucas replied. *He's mean. He shouts at the kids when we play too loud.*

I don't like mean grown-ups. We should get him back.

I don't know. He's scary.

Her eyes darkened. *Awww, is little Lucas scared? I'm not scared of him, and I'm just a girl.*

I'm not scared! Lucas insisted.

Prove it.

What do you want me to do?

I want to see how quiet you can be.

Lucas got to his feet. *Quiet as a ghost! My mother says so!*

All right then. Take this.

Lourdes opened her fist to reveal a small object nestled in her palm, although Lucas would have sworn both her hands were completely empty only moments ago. She offered it to him.

A folded penknife.

Lucas reached for the knife, then hesitated. *I'm not supposed to play with knives. I'm too small.*

Just like I thought. A little baby.

I'm not!

He snatched the knife away from her grasp, then carefully unfolded it. The blade was keen and bright, gleaming in the sunlight like a poisonous tooth.

Lourdes put her arm around his shoulders and pulled him close as she began to whisper. *Now, listen while I tell you the game. I want you to sneak over there to those trees, to where that nasty Francisco is sleeping. But remember, you mustn't make a sound, because if you wake him, the game is ruined. Understand?*

Lucas nodded. He was a good, obedient boy. His father always said so.

You have to get in really close, Lucas. Close enough to smell the wine on his breath. Then, once you're there, I want you to take the knife and pull it across his throat, just like this.

She extended one finger, and drew it swiftly across her carotid.

Lucas' breath caught in his throat. *But...*

Her hand tightened on his shoulder. *Think about how mean he's always been to you and the other children, Lucas. Everyone will think you're a big, brave hero. There's really nothing to it. Just imagine you're slicing yourself a nice piece of cake.*

And despite his deep-seated panic and revulsion, when it came down to it, he could not refuse her. As hard as Lucas tried to visualise the disapproving faces of his parents, who had always told him not to play with sharp things, and *never* to hurt other people, even if they were mean and nasty, Lourdes' insistent whisper pushed everything else out of his mind, like thick black smoke filling a room.

So the little boy did exactly as he was told. He crept over to the trees, knelt down by the unconscious drunk, and after a moment's hesitation, lifted the blade and swiftly opened Francisco's throat.

There was a great deal of blood. Lucas found he had to quickly jump out of the way, lest it splash on his shoes.

But after Francisco had ceased his kicking and gurgling, his reddened eyes staring accusingly up at his small assassin, Lucas thought for a moment and had to admit Lourdes had been right. It was a *very* good game. Much better than killing stupid ants.

The girl appeared at his side. She leant down and kissed his cheek. *You're brilliant at this, Lucas.*

He flushed, quietly ecstatic at her praise.

Now let's go and tell the other kids, she suggested. *I bet they'll want to join in too.*

And they did. The popularity of the new game quickly spread amongst the children, and by sunset that day, only a handful of adults were left alive on the island. Soon, the children began to grow restless. With no grown-ups around, there was no one to stop their games, but also no one to play with.

Then the English couple arrived from the mainland, visiting Almanzora on a day trip.

They wandered the empty streets in bafflement, shouting in the same tone of annoyed frustration that came so readily to all English tourists abroad, as though bellowing ever more loudly would serve to make them better understood.

Lourdes was the first to introduce herself to the visitors. The English woman was pregnant, close to term, and allowed the girl to caress her swollen belly. Lourdes leant in and whispered to the unborn child, inviting it to take part in their game.

Within hours the woman was dead. Her husband managed to survive a little longer, even managing to gun down a number of his tormentors, but that was all part of the fun. In the end, he was shot by police while attempting to defend himself against the children; all the authorities saw was a murderous lunatic and acted accordingly.

Of course, the children were only too eager to play with them too.

Afterwards, Lucas followed a number of them as they crowded onto the boat belonging to the policemen. There was no fun left to be had on the island, so they would have to go and play elsewhere. A couple of the older boys knew how to sail and piloted the vessel safely across to the mainland.

But upon their arrival, they found that Lourdes had vanished as suddenly as she had first appeared, even though they were certain she had been onboard when they first set out on their journey. Without her guileful encouragement, the allure of the game faded.

The scale of the city port was overwhelming in comparison to their small island town, and even if they found other children to join in with their fun, they could not possibly hurt all of the thousands of grown-ups that thronged the streets.

Some of them decided to turn around and go back to the island, but Lucas could not bring himself to accompany them. Caught up in the thrill of the game, he had watched calmly from the sidelines as some of the older kids stormed into his parents's house and played with them, but suddenly he found that he missed his mother and father terribly. The thought of going back to his house and finding them there, their lifeless faces bloated and black with swarming flies, terrified him.

Perhaps if he set out on his own, Lourdes would find him again. *She* always knew what to do.

He lived rough for a time, eventually finding his way out of the city and into the countryside, living on fruit picked from trees and bushes and whatever other food he could forage. He was small, and alone, and often frightened – but he survived. Eventually, he made his way across the border into France, where was picked up on the roadside by a passing couple, the Medevs. They were older in years, and childless, and they soon decided to take the little lost boy in and raise him as their own.

Away from Lourdes' influence, Lucas was once again the same harmless child he had always been, and took happily to his new life. As the years passed, he grew to manhood, and the events on the island gradually took on the semblance of a fever dream; fervid, distorted imaginings that his adult mind dismissed as childish delusion. He never spoke of them to anyone, although in times of stress he would often glimpse half-forgotten faces in nightmares: Francisco, his birth parents, Lourdes.

Always Lourdes.

In time, he met a beautiful girl, Clémentine, and fell in love. Looking for teaching work, she was offered a job in a French school near Bucharest, and Lucas, still driven by a nameless urge to keep moving, was content to accompany her. By now, his adopted parents had both passed on, leaving him a small inheritance, and he decided he wanted to try and put down some of his childhood memories in the form of a novel. Perhaps then the dreams would stop.

He decided he would call it *Who Can Kill A Child?*

They moved into an old manor house, surrounded by wild Romanian countryside, and commenced their new life. Clémentine would return home from school each day and find Lucas hunched over his laptop, his mind off in some faraway place. Watching him work, she often thought to herself that he still possessed the eyes of a young boy.

Tell me about your book, she asked him one summer's evening, as they lay curled in each other's arms.

It's a horror novel, he replied.

Clémentine groaned in dismay. *I don't know who would want to read stuff like that*, she said. *Can such terrible things really happen?*

Not to us, Lucas said, and pulled her close to him.

One night, not long afterwards, the children came to their home and gleefully proved him a liar, lunging out of the darkness as though they had erupted directly from Lucas' own nightmares. Clémentine was utterly terrified, could not comprehend what was happening, and Lucas knew she would never understand if he tried to explain that the children only wanted to play with them.

They fled the house and took refuge in a nearby sewer system, abandoned for some years. But Lucas had already been injured in the initial attack, and their pursuers were smaller, faster, better suited to the narrow concrete tunnels. The couple did not stand a chance.

Trapped, they attempted to escape via the only route possible, a metal ladder mounted in the wall, but one of the children surprised Lucas when he was halfway up and sent him crashing to the ground below, smashing his spine.

The other kids dragged him away, abandoning him in a side tunnel. He wanted to tell them, *I understand, I was like you once, I played this game too!* But he could not speak, could not move, could not do anything but lie there and remember.

And then he heard it: the hollow sound of rubber smacking against concrete, echoing around the tunnels. It put Lucas in mind of an angry parent repeatedly slapping a child.

A small, lithe figure emerged from the shadows, bouncing a ball against the floor. She was unchanged by the passage of time, still beautiful beyond her years. As Lourdes moved closer, staring impassively down at him, Lucas thought he could still discern a beatific glow to her features, despite the clammy gloom of their underground surroundings. He thought back to the brilliant, hot day upon which they had first met, and was struck by the sudden realisation that he would never see the sun again.

Nevertheless, he wanted to tell her how happy he was she had found him after all these years, so many hundreds of miles from the Mediterranean island where they had originally become friends. But when he tried to speak, he could only manage to feebly croak her name.

She smirked. *Oh, but didn't I tell you? That isn't my real name,* she said, adding as a sly afterthought, *Although my real name does start with an 'L'.*

Lucas gazed dumbly back at her. The girl thought for a moment, and then grew animated. *I know another game we can play,* she said. *I'll show you my true face, the face I wear underneath this one, and you can try and guess my real name.*

So she did.

And once he had finished screaming, Lucas finally understood everything.

Dean Corso

Johnny Depp in *The Ninth Gate*, 1999
written by John Brownjohn, Enrique Urbizu
and Roman Polanski
based on the book by Arturo Pérez-Reverte
directed by Roman Polanski

Corso stood trembling before the gate. This was it: everything he had fought and schemed and betrayed to get. If he had stopped short of committing outright murder, it was only because he was an inveterate coward by nature. Ultimate knowledge, ultimate power, would soon be his.

He thought back to Boris Balkan's last moments before the flames consumed him; the man's habitually smug arrogance turning to agonised terror as the realisation of his own failure dawned. Balkan had dedicated a small fortune and an entire lifetime to his obsessive quest for Satanic omnipotence, only to suffer the exact same fate as his idol Aristede Torchia: his flesh scorched to brittle charcoal, his cherished dreams turned to ashes.

Balkan and his ilk would never understand one simple truth; that all the money and the power in the world meant little if you did not possess a particular talent for the well-timed manoeuvre. Corso, on the other hand, had always prided himself on his ability to be in the right place at the right time; many of his most lucrative coups had come about simply because of his quicksilver wits and unerring instincts.

That and an admittedly sizeable amount of good fortune. His father had always told him he possessed the luck of the Devil; now, Corso supposed he was finally about to put that theory to the test.

Of course, a certain lack of scruples had also played a part; a quality his father could also attest to, the teenaged Corso having sold the entirety of the man's rare book collection and absconded with the proceeds while Corso senior was enjoying an illicit weekend away with his mistress.

But his father was long dead, as was everyone who had made the error of getting too close to Dean Corso. Bernie Rothstein was the nearest thing to a friend he'd ever had, until Corso had discovered him strung up in his bookshop, the first victim of the deadly chain of events that had resulted in the deaths of several other not-so-innocent parties, and which had finally brought the unscrupulous book dealer here, standing before a fabled gateway that led to...where?

No one really knew for sure; as was always the case when you dealt with the Devil, lies and evasions were the only currency He recognised.

Well, Corso liked to think he knew a thing or two about such transactions too. But doubts still plagued him. Did he seriously intend to match his wits against the Prince of Darkness? For all his feral cunning, the book dealer was strictly a small-time hustler; could he possibly hope to come out ahead against the greatest con artist in existence?

He fumbled for his packet of Lucky Strikes and lit one, considering his next play. When all was said and done, what was left for him back in New York? Everyone was dead. And could he really go back to his old life, after all he'd witnessed? Corso, who'd never previously believed in anything but himself, had undergone a drastic conversion over the course of the previous few days. It might not have been strictly correct to label it *Damascene*, but nevertheless, he had come to embrace a devout, unquestioning faith...of sorts.

What the hell, he muttered, and stepped through the gate.

He emerged into a blindingly white room. It was covered from floor to ceiling in spotlessly-bleached tiles, pure as virgin snow. Corso blinked owlishly behind his spectacles, his eyes adjusting to the sudden glare. Could *this* be Hell? It looked more like a county morgue.

A figure emerged out of the whiteness: a young girl, cradling a ball in her arms. She, too, was dressed in entirely in white, as though she had been formed out of the very walls themselves. Her hair was golden, her cherubic features flawless. So religiously kitsch was her appearance that Corso decided all she was lacking was a golden harp and set of feathered wings protruding from her back.

Some terrible error had been made, clearly.

Hello, Corso, she said.

Excuse me, I...think I must be in the wrong place, Corso stammered.

Oh no. You're precisely where you wished to be.

Corso gazed around, ever more confused. *So, this is...?*

The girl nodded. *An entrance hallway, at least. I*

find it helps to show up the stains more clearly. Gives me a sense of what work needs to be done.

Corso chose not to dwell on the implications of this. *So you're...?*

She smiled, and then he glimpsed it. A hint of something ageless and dreadful concealed behind that perfect face. His skin prickled, as though stung by a million tiny needles. Instinctively, he fumbled for his cigarettes.

You already have one lit, the girl said gravely.

Corso's cheeks burned. He felt ashamed of appearing so gauche in the company of so illustrious a presence.

Of course, how stupid of me, he said, and plucked the half-smoked cigarette from his mouth, tapping the ashes into his palm for fear of soiling his immaculate surroundings.

The girl looked bored. *Right, enough of the preliminaries,* She said. *You have done remarkably well to get this far, but one small task remains before you can receive your ultimate reward.*

Another task? Hadn't he done enough already? Corso hurriedly reminded himself that he didn't make the rules around here. *What is it?* he asked.

It should be no trouble at all for a man of your talents. Normally I wouldn't even ask, but seeing as you're so very well-suited to the job. Her eyes gleamed with malign amusement. *I need you to obtain a book.*

Corso groaned inwardly. Another goddamned book!

Frankly, he longed to be finished with the whole miserable business. Yes, books had been good to him, but if he were being entirely truthful, Corso was sick to death of them. Fiction, non-fiction, they were all equally interminable. Like the true cynic he was, the dealer knew the price of everything and the value of nothing. Books had only ever been a means to an end, nothing more. Faced with a quiet evening at home, Corso would much rather spend it finishing a bottle of scotch than a good book.

He said none of this aloud. Instead, he simply asked: *What book?*

It's called The Three Mothers. *Written by an alchemist named Varelli.*

He knew it, of course. *It's not a particularly rare item. I believe several copies are in circulation.*

She wagged her finger in admonishment. *That's where you're mistaken, Corso. The subjects of the book have taken great pains to remove all copies from the public domain, by whatever means necessary.*

The subjects...?

The Three Mothers themselves. Mater Suspiriorum, Mater Tenebrarum, and Mater Lachrymarum.

Corso knew the legend. Three witch sisters whose insidious influence had spread throughout the world like a cancer. Up until a few days ago he would have dismissed it as just another spook story, but recent events had gone some way towards convincing Corso that even the most far-fetched of such tales often possessed a certain unfortunate truth to them.

Why do you need the book?

The Mothers jealously guard their secrets. Even I know very little of real worth about them. Varelli, however, was famously indiscreet in what he set down in the book. I require that knowledge.

Even the Devil needs to get one up on the other guy every now and then, right?

The girl's eyes met his. Their dark pupils seemed to expand across the white sclerae, like ink in water. For an instant, Corso felt as though he were drowning in a freezing black ocean. *I do not appreciate challenges to my authority,* She said, her implacable tone no less threatening for the girlish voice that delivered it.

Corso decided there was an undeniable irony in that statement, given exactly who was making it, but kept such indelicate observations to himself. Instead, he wearily accepted this latest challenge – really, what other choice did he have? – and within hours, was boarding a plane to London.

The girl had informed him of a copy of Varelli's book that could be located there, in the private library of an eminent occultist named Lorimer Van Helsing. The man himself had mysteriously vanished some decades before, but his granddaughter Jessica still acted as custodian of his legacy.

She's a complete shut-in, the girl had warned him. *A middle-aged lush. A man of your particular talents should have no trouble with her.*

The Devil already knew him far too well, it appeared. *Why can't you just take the book for yourself?*

Her grandfather was a knowledgable man. Cautious. The house is well-protected against incursions from other planes.

But not against light-fingered book dealers bearing gifts, apparently.

Upon disembarking at Heathrow, Corso picked up a couple of bottles of Johnny Walker Blue, then made his way towards the exit, intending to take a cab directly to Central London. But before he could get to the taxi rank, he was intercepted by a familiar face: the nameless lynx-eyed woman who had served as his escort and bodyguard throughout the whole affair of the Ninth Gate.

The same young woman whom he had last seen writhing naked on top of him, her features contorted in infernal ecstasy.

Hello again, Corso, she said.

I, ah, wasn't expecting to see you again, he stammered.

An inscrutable smile. *Is this going to be one of those awkward morning-after conversations?*

She led him to a parked rental car. Corso thought of asking her what she was doing there, but supposed the Devil was merely protecting his investment. He pretended to doze for the duration of their journey to Kensington.

When they pulled up outside the townhouse belonging to the Van Helsing woman, Corso grabbed his luggage and climbed out of the car. *I don't know exactly how long this will take,* he told his driver.

Knowing you, not too long, she replied, and sped off before he could ask exactly what she meant.

Returning his attention to the task at hand, Corso mounted the steps to the front door. An intercom had been installed besides the entrance, and he pressed the call button firmly, keeping his finger on it long enough to make the necessary point.

Eventually, the intercom spat back a curt reply. *Who are you?*

The female voice was clipped and plummy, but coarse with the residue of too much booze, too many cigarettes.

Corso leant forward. *My name is Dean Corso. I'm an, ah, academic researcher. I was wondering if I—*

Fuck off.

So much for the Brits not saying what they meant. He tried again. *Am I speaking to Ms Jessica Van Helsing?*

Fucking fuck off, I said.

He held up his duty free bag in view of the

intercom camera and waggled it insinuatingly. *Look, all I wanted to do was have a little drink and a chat...*

Silence for a moment, then the lock buzzed, allowing him entry to the house.

Inside, the front hallway was dark. Corso could taste damp and dust on his tongue, hanging thickly in the air. He looked around. The house's décor was doubtless impeccable once, but had been allowed to atrophy and decay.

A tall figure stepped out of the shadows: Jessica Van Helsing. Something small glinted in her right hand. A pistol, aimed at his chest. *Who are you?*

Corso raised his hands. *I told you, I'm just a researcher. My name is Dean Corso.*

Identification?

He sought permission to reach inside his jacket pocket, and once it was granted, gingerly produced his passport.

Jessica took the document from his hand, keeping her weapon trained on him the whole time. As she inspected it, Corso took the opportunity to covertly inspect her. She had been beautiful once, he could tell; tall and aristocratic, the product of what the English called *good breeding*. But her once-lithe limbs had grown scrawny, her rosy flesh lined and jaundiced. What had happened to make her like this?

She snapped the passport closed. *It could be fake.*

Corso shrugged helplessly. *Well, I can assure you that the whisky isn't.*

Let's see, shall we?

Motioning with the gun, Jessica guided him through into a book-lined study, curtains closed against the outside world. The desk that dominated the room was lined with empty booze bottles and glasses. An overflowing ashtray sat over to one side, containing enough grey ash that Corso half-suspected an entire human body had been cremated there.

His captor instructed him to place his hands against the wall while she patted him down and searched for concealed weapons. Already finding the woman's constant paranoia tedious, Corso looked away and, out of sheer habit, immediately began scanning the titles on the bookshelves. Mostly esoterica, some of it worth a considerable sum. The books were the only thing he'd seen in the house that showed any evidence of care and upkeep; the spines were undamaged, the shelves kept assiduously dust-free.

This was my grandfather's room, Jessica murmured, registering his interest. *The books are all I have left of him. He disappeared when I was younger.*

What happened?

They took him. He was on a lecture tour in Romania in the 1970s, and he just vanished. She let out a bitter laugh, almost a snarl. *But don't pretend you don't know.*

Corso attempted an innocent look; a mode of expression that did not come at all naturally to him. *I swear to you, I'm just looking for a particular book.*

He proffered one of the whisky bottles, a peace offering. Jessica snatched it away from him, then carefully began to check the seal for signs of tampering. Corso suppressed an exasperated sigh.

Apparently satisfied, she opened the bottle, then selected two glasses from amongst those arrayed on the desk before her. She splashed a generous measure into both tumblers, then held one out to him. *You first.*

Given the unwashed state of the glasses, Corso felt as though he were the one in far greater danger of being poisoned, but he bit his tongue and took a generous swallow of the alcohol.

Happy now? he asked his host.

Jessica merely growled and motioned for him to sit. She rapidly drained her glass and poured herself another, not bothering to extend the courtesy to Corso. *You mentioned something about a book?* she said.

It's called The Three Mothers. *I'm currently researching their legend, and I believe there is a copy in your grandfather's collection.*

Jessica crossed to the shelves, where she immediately located the volume in question. Opening it to the title page, her eyes grew haunted. *What do you know about them?* she finally asked Corso.

Very little, if I'm being honest.

She slammed the book closed. *You should keep it that way.*

Returning to the desk, she opened a drawer and placed the book inside. Seeing Corso's expression, Jessica gave a smile that was like a wire slicing into the flesh of her face. *I don't let just anybody get their grubby paws on Grandfather's books, you know. So, why don't we get to know each other a little first?*

Before too much longer, they'd finished one bottle of whisky and started on the second. The drunker she got, the more loquacious Jessica became. Corso feigned interest as she explained to him in great detail about the Van Helsing family and their illustrious history as vampire hunters. By the time she got to the subject of her grandfather's disappearance, Corso had quietly concluded that the woman was completely mad. She blamed his abduction on the British security services, for reasons the dealer couldn't quite fathom.

Corso decided he needed to put a swift end to the conversation by any means necessary, before he ended up losing his own mind. Getting up from his chair, he crossed to where Jessica was sitting, leant down, and drew her face to his.

Judging by her hungry response, he guessed she had not been touched by a man in a very long time.

Later, as they lay together in bed, Jessica snoring softly beside him, Corso fought the urge to sleep himself. His head was clotted, thudding dully with sexual exertion and an incipient hangover. But remembering the little girl and her bottomless black eyes, he at last mustered the energy to climb out of bed. Careful not to wake his erstwhile lover, he pulled on his clothes and eased his way from the bedroom.

Downstairs, he quickly drank some water, then grabbed his coat and bag. Moving to the study, he went immediately to the desk and removed the copy of Varelli's book from the drawer. Now, Corso could deliver the Devil His prize and finally claim his own reward in return.

He was halfway through the front door when he heard the telltale click of a pistol hammer being cocked.

You little shit.

Jessica stood naked in the hallway, her weapon raised in readiness.

Corso raised his hands. *I swear, I was going to bring it back. I just needed—*

Balls. I knew you were a liar the moment I clapped eyes on you. Never trust a man with a fucking goatee.

Faced with such impeccable, inarguable logic, Corso did the only thing he could: he ran.

As he dashed down the townhouse steps, he heard the gun's report and felt a shot whizz by his ear. Luckily, he presented a moving target, and his pursuer was a dipsomaniac with a bad case of the DTs. All he needed to do was keep on moving, very rapidly indeed.

Corso scrambled into the street, only to hear another shot ricochet off concrete. Although he doubted Jessica's aim, he would rather not give her too many more opportunities to test it. But where could he run to?

At that moment, a familiar rental car skidded into view, and a door was flung open. Inside, the young woman called out to him: *Get in!*

Corso flung himself inside, and the vehicle screeched safely away. Glancing down at the wing mirror, the dealer watched as the naked woman receding behind them stood in the street yelling obscenities and firing shots wildly into the air.

You certainly have a way with women, Corso, his rescuer remarked.

He slumped tiredly in his seat. *Just take me straight back to Heathrow. I need to catch the next flight to Paris.*

Do you have it?

Corso fumbled in his bag and held the volume aloft in enervated triumph. *And believe me, I never want to see another fucking book again after this.*

Oh, I can certainly help you with that...

The young woman tore the book from his hand.

Corso sat up, blinking. *What are you doing?*

Her eyes flashed an unearthly green. *There's a war coming, Corso, and I'm changing sides.* Before he knew it, she had lunged across his lap and opened the passenger door. *Goodbye, lover.*

One swift kick was all it took to expel him from the moving vehicle. Corso's last thought before the world went dark was that it might be time to start reconsidering his lifelong scepticism towards the value of trust in everyday human interactions.

When he awoke, he found himself lying on an old leather settee. Lifting up his head, he looked around, bewildered. He was in a large library room, surrounded by yet more damned books, thousands of them. Corso quickly surmised that any building housing such a collection must be old and impossibly grand, and yet, despite the fact that the house was obviously inhabited, he still perceived an atmosphere of abandonment, as though no living soul had walked here for decades. The air felt unpleasantly dank, suffused with rot, and a heavy silence lay over the library like a net, preventing any living sound from escaping.

Corso sat up and frantically brushed himself off, unable to rid himself of the nagging delusion that mould was forming on his clothes. He coughed, trying to expel the fouly acrid taste that coated the inside of his mouth. He desperately needed a drink, a cigarette, anything.

At that moment, the door to the library opened, revealing a bald man dressed in a majordomo's uniform. Upon finding Corso awake, the man smiled. Incongruously, he produced a child's lollipop and began to suck it, the candy appearing ludicrously small and dainty in his white-gloved hand.

Corso, he said.

Who are you? Corso demanded. *Where the hell am I?*

The majordomo laughed. *I'm Leandro. But we've met before, quite recently in fact. Surely you remember?*

Corso stared at the man. He'd never seen him before in his life, but there was something in his eyes, a familiar sardonic twinkle...

He realised. *It's you.*

A nod.

Why the penguin suit?

A mocking bow. *I am but your humble servant.*

Look, I'm sorry about the book. That bitch double-crossed me. I can get it back...

Leandro raised a solitary finger, silencing him. *She will be dealt with.*

And what about me?

You are precisely where you need to be.

Corso got to his feet. *Which is where, exactly? What is this place?*

Leandro reached down and fastidiously brushed a smear of dirt from Corso's coat. *You are free to look around at your leisure. There are others here like you. You'll have plenty of time to get acquainted.*

The dealer suddenly felt hollow inside, as though a plug had been pulled in his belly, sending his innards spilling to the floor.

What about my reward? he asked desperately. *I did everything you asked! I solved the riddle of the Ninth Gate! Balkan couldn't do it but I did!*

I promised you knowledge, did I not?

Yes!

Leandro motioned around him. *Well, the shelves are brimming with it.*

The walls seemed to close in around Corso, threatening to bury him in an avalanche of books, suffocating him with the weight of the wisdom he'd sought. *That's...that's not...*

We've needed an archivist here for quite some time. You seem eminently well-suited to the task.

No! Corso's skin crawled at the thought of it.

Dinner will be served at eight. Will there be anything else, sir?

The dealer slumped back down to the settee, beaten. *Is there whisky at least? And cigarettes?*

I'm sure I can arrange something, Leandro purred.

The majordomo turned to leave, then paused to pluck a thick volume from a nearby shelf. Holding it reverently in both hands, he brought it over to Corso.

This might be a good place to start. I'm told it's a real page-turner.

Corso took the proffered book, and glanced down at the cover. The Holy Bible.

When he looked up again, the majordomo was gone, although the sound of his dry laughter still hung in the air, like poison spores.

Settling back on the couch, Corso resignedly turned to the Book of Genesis and began to read.

Justine

Garance Marillier in *Grave*
(*Raw*), 2016
written & directed by
Julia Ducournau

Justine stared at the livid scars criss-crossing her father's chest, tracing a scabrous map of pain and desire.

Her mother. This had all started with her mother.

The awful hunger that gripped Justine, the same cannibalistic craving that had driven her sister Alexia to kill; this had been their mother's genetic gift to them. Anthropophagy: a dominant trait, like brown eyes or webbed fingers. After all, what could possibly be more dominant than to slaughter and devour your fellow beings?

But there was still so much she didn't understand. She gazed imploringly at her father, searching his face for answers, but finding only a hopelessly forlorn sympathy.

Ask your mother, was all he could offer her.

Justine turned to find her mother standing in the doorway. At the sight of the woman's face, she suddenly realised she hated her. She imagined battering it to a fleshy pulp, reducing those delicate features to their raw constituents, nothing but blood and bone and meat, a scarlet feast. She fantasised about tearing into her mother's face with her teeth, greedily licking the dark lifeblood from her fingertips. Perhaps then, the terrible emptiness inside her would finally be sated.

Her mother smiled. Justine wondered how much the woman could read in her eyes.

Why? she said, simply.

You and I need to take a trip, her mother replied. *It's high time you met my Mother.*

Justine was confused. *But grand-maman died years ago.*

Not my birth mother. There are far deeper ties than blood.

Who is this woman? A foster mother? Justine looked over to her father, who immediately averted his eyes, saying nothing.

Her mother moved to Justine's side and affectionately kissed her forehead.

Of a sort. She has no children of her own, but

there are legions of us who are honoured to call her Mother.

Every cryptic statement provoked yet more questions, but Justine's baffled inquiries were cut short when the older woman gently placed a quietening finger upon her daughter's lips.

We'll leave in the morning, her mother said, and that was the end of it.

Justine slept fitfully that night. It took her hours to fall asleep, and even after she did, she dreamt that she was still awake, lying paralysed in bed, unable to do so much as blink an eye. In her dream, a mysterious woman came to visit her in her room. The visitor was beautiful, blonde and slim and inexpressibly fragile, like an origami flower you could crush between your fingers.

Who are you? Justine asked her.

My name is Silvia Hacherman, the woman replied. *I knew your mother when she was just a little girl. We lived in the same apartment building in Rome.*

My mother lived in Rome?

When she was very small.

She never told me.

There is so much she hasn't told you, Justine.

I want to know everything! Justine pleaded.

Silvia smiled sadly, and silently lifted her blouse to expose her bare abdomen. Her belly had been torn open, and her stomach cavity emptied. Justine stared mutely into the bloody hole, unable to look away.

I had to kill my own mother, Silvia murmured. *But sometimes that's for the best.*

Justine wanted to admit that she, too, had entertained such thoughts, but found she could not respond. Her tongue felt like a withered dead thing on the floor of her mouth.

After a few more moments, Silvia let the blouse drop, hiding her dreadful emptiness from view. *Once we used to eat our enemies, now we study to become veterinarians,* she told Justine, then slowly drifted from the room.

The next morning, after Justine and her mother had loaded their bags into the car and set out on their journey, Justine whispered Silvia's parting statement to herself, trying to make sense of it.

Her mother looked at her sharply. *What was that?*

Nothing. Just something from a dream I had last night.

Her mother's eyes lingered on her for a moment, but she said nothing more. After she had turned her attention back to the road, Justine finally asked her: *Where are we going?*

To Rome, her mother replied.

Justine's breath caught in her chest. She could not speak for a moment, the image of Silvia's ruined torso imprinted upon her imagination. She screwed her eyes shut, attempting to banish the bloody picture from her mind.

When she was eventually able to speak again, she said in a small voice: *Have you ever been to Rome before?*

We lived there when I was very young, her mother said.

Does your Mother live there too?

Yes.

Does she—?

We'll stop over in Milan tonight, her mother said, still avoiding Justine's questions. *We'll get ourselves a good night's rest, and it won't take too much longer from there tomorrow.*

Justine stayed silent for the remainder of the day's journey. That night in the motel, Justine's mother sleeping soundly in the adjacent bed, Justine dreamt of Silvia again.

This time, she dreamed she was in a room deep underground, crowded with people. The subterranean air was chill, the only warmth coming from the body heat of those clustered around her. She recognised none of them, but knew implicitly that they were all gathered together in some nameless, unspeakable commonality.

Looking down, Justine saw that Silvia lay naked and helpless on a slab before them. Upon seeing the woman's frail body, shivering with fear and anticipation, Justine felt herself beginning to drool uncontrollably, warm saliva spilling down her chin. Horrified, she tried to back away from the slab, but was unable to force her way through the densely-packed huddle that surrounded her.

Silvia looked up at her. *It's what your Mother wants*, she told Justine.

But I'm a vegetarian, Justine replied stupidly. *So is she.*

Not your birth mother. There are deeper ties than blood. Taste it and you'll see.

Suddenly the assembled congregation were jostling forward, eagerly grabbing at Silvia's flawlessly nude body. Despite her undoubted beauty, it was not simple sexual desire that motivated them, but an even more base compulsion. Their fingers tore into her pale flesh, opening up the meat of her body to the cold air. Justine found herself at the mercy of the horde's collective hunger, compelled to lunge in and voraciously taste Silvia for herself.

But as her hands reached greedily down to seize whatever delicious morsel she could scavenge for herself, Justine suddenly found herself lying on her back, staring up at the rapacious throng huddled around her, their hands and faces brightly painted with her blood.

Now, she *was* Silvia, and as the pack continued their feast, Justine found she could feel every tear, every bite, every last shred of her being relentlessly, agonisingly ripped away.

She awoke with a choked scream, the cry lodging in her throat like an edged bone.

Darling, what is it? Her mother was immediately awake and at her bedside.

Justine pushed her away and made a dash for the bathroom, managing to hurl herself down in front of the toilet moments before she was violently sick. Swept helplessly along by a

- 93 -

torrent of nausea, Justine was dimly aware of her mother kneeling beside her, holding her long hair back from her face.

Finally, the sickness passed. Justine lay her cheek against the cool porcelain of the toilet rim while her mother gently stroked her head. Her stomach voided, she found she could no longer hold back the words that demanded to be spoken aloud.

Who is Silvia Hacherman? she finally asked.

Her mother's hand paused in its soothing motion, the fingers curling around a lock of Justine's hair. Justine thought for an instant her mother might tear the hair from her scalp, but after a few moments, her grip relaxed.

How do you know that name? her mother replied in a hushed tone.

She came to me in my dreams.

Her mother sighed. When she spoke again, her voice was slow with reluctance. *Mother demanded an offering. Silvia was chosen.*

Justine raised her head and rounded on her parent. *You ate her alive!*

I was only a child, Justine. It was my induction. That was the night I was first introduced to Mother. After that, I was hers forever.

Who is this Mother? What sort of mother demands such atrocities?

The older woman's voice dropped to a reverent whisper.

Her name is Mater Lachrymarum...

Once Justine was safely back in bed, her mother told her everything, the words spilling out as if from an open wound. That was the night Justine first learned of the legend of the Mother of Tears and her two terrible sisters, who had each dwelled in separate cities until two of their secret lairs had been destroyed; of the nefarious army they controlled from their sole remaining house in Rome; and of the imminent conflict that loomed over them all like a burgeoning tempest, a rancorous war for control that threatened to consume the entire world.

The stories her mother told her were incredible; no, more than that, *insane,* but Justine nevertheless found that she did not doubt a single word. A calm acceptance washed over her like a baptism; over the course of recent weeks she had participated in unspeakable acts of cannibalism and murder without ever truly understanding *why* – but now, at last, she had been gifted with a rationale for her actions, an explanation for everything that was vile and grotesque in her life, however fantastical it might have seemed.

When her mother finished speaking, she suggested they both got some more rest before continuing on their journey the next day. Her mind teeming with shadows, Justine was certain she would be unable to sleep, but after her mother turned the lights off, oblivion quickly claimed her regardless, and the remainder of her slumber that night was no longer troubled by dreams of the doomed Silvia Hacherman.

Mother and daughter both slept until late the next morning, and awoke refreshed. After a light breakfast of fruit and cereal, they resumed their long drive towards Rome. Now that Justine's mother had at last revealed the truth to her daughter, she seemed far easier in her own skin, and gaily joked and chatted for the remainder of the journey. For her part, Justine did her best to engage in conversation, but found herself assailed by a grim sense of foreboding.

Now, she could finally recognise that her

whole life had been a steady progression towards an unknowable darkness, but of what might lie on the other side of that darkness – if anything even *did* – she was still helplessly, hopelessly ignorant.

When they eventually reached Rome's outskirts, Justine feared they might become entangled in the chaotic snarl of traffic that twisted through the narrow streets like wild jungle vines, but her mother navigated the roads with easy assurance, as though she were being guided by a trail of twine through a labyrinth.

Before long, they pulled up in a large city square, outside a grand old building announcing itself as the Hotel Levana.

Justine turned to her mother. *Are we taking a room here? I thought—*

Shhhh. You'll see, was all the older woman said in reply.

She led Justine inside. The hotel's lobby was awash with cerulean light, almost liquid in its quality. The walls were papered with ornate swirls of turquoise and aquamarine, and the lobby furniture upholstered with thick, blue velvet.

Stepping into the building was very much like drowning, Justine decided.

Justine's mother summoned a nearby porter. The interaction that followed was practically wordless; the man merely looked at them both, nodded, and quietly asked the two women to follow him, escorting them to one of the hotel elevators. Inside, he pressed the button for the ground floor once, paused, and pressed it twice again.

The elevator doors closed with a sound that was almost a sigh. Justine felt the lift begin to descend into the depths of the building, even though there were no lower levels listed on either the floor indicator or the operating panel. When the mechanism eventually ground to a halt and the doors reopened, the porter gestured for mother and daughter to step out, but did not exit the car himself. Justine turned and watched him as the doors slid closed once more, and thought she glimpsed the faintest trace of a smile haunting his face in the brief moments before he vanished from sight.

They found themselves in a candlelit antechamber, devoid of furnishings save for a large canvas that hung on one wall: an oil portrait of a nude woman, exquisite in her consummate beauty. Justine's studies had always been science-focused, and she knew next to nothing about art, but the painting stirred something in her regardless; a nascent sense of awe, and perhaps even terror. She understood there could be no secrets from a being of such absolute divinity, if one even existed. Such an entity could not possibly be resisted, or denied.

Beautiful, isn't she? Justine's mother said.

Justine said nothing; however, the word that instinctively came to her tongue was not *beautiful*, but *dreadful*.

A closed set of double doors awaited them on the far side of the chamber. As Justine's mother began to lead her towards them, Justine resisted.

What do I do? she asked her mother.

You'll know when the time comes, the older woman replied.

Taking Justine's arm, she steered her daughter towards the doorway. When her mother's hands reached down to turn the door handles, Justine could see that they were trembling.

The doors opened, admitting them into a large darkened room. So dark was it that Justine could not discern any physical limit to the impenetrable blackness that stretched away on all sides; it was as though the infinite entirety of the universe was contained in this solitary space.

There was a single source of illumination in the chamber, a light suspended above an ornately carved wooden chair, upon which sat the very woman whose likeness Justine had just glimpsed in the painting displayed outside. She wore a flowing robe of the deepest blue, as fathomless as an ocean. Indeed, the folds of the material seemed to eddy and swirl as Justine looked at them; the woman did not wear the robe so much as let it wash over her like a restless sea.

Made giddy by the illusion – if illusion it was – Justine glanced away, up into the woman's eyes, and gasped.

Despite the evident skill of the portrait, it could not hope to capture the full magnitude of its subject; to look upon the Mother of Tears was to behold a vast, towering tsunami, awesome in its sheer elemental ferocity, irresistible in its power. For Justine, to stare into the numbing depths of the woman's gaze was to confront her own complete and utter insignificance.

Shuddering, the younger woman understood that she could be instantly swept away with but the merest wave of the Mother's hand.

Lachrymarum.

Gradually, she also became aware of two other presences in the chamber. The first she glimpsed only as a lurking shadow, lingering close to the woman in the chair, pulling the darkness around itself like a thick blanket. Justine could not discern anything of the figure's features, but felt the frigid sting of cruel eyes studying her.

Tenebrarum.

The second presence, she came to realise, was all about her, bodiless and incorporeal, drifting to fill the space like a mist. If Justine listened hard enough, she thought she could hear it whispering to her in a voice like a thousand vipers.

Suspiriorum.

Justine's parent stepped forward. *Mothers*, she said.

You have returned to us, the Mother of Tears replied.

Justine's mother bowed her head. *I bore two children of my own. One daughter was unable to control the appetites I passed onto her. But Justine may be of use to you in the war ahead. I offer her to you as a token of my loyalty.*

The Mother's gaze shifted to Justine. The effect of her undivided attention was such that Justine felt as though she were standing over an open grave, its cold depths yawning emptily before her. She shivered, and clasped her arms tightly around herself.

And what does the girl have to say for herself? Mater Lachrymarum asked.

Justine forced herself to look the Mother of Tears in the eye.

I don't know why I'm here, she said finally. *I don't understand anything. My mother lied to me and my sister our entire lives.*

Justine! her mother hissed.

Justine ignored her. *I don't know who you are,* she told Mater Lachrymarum. *I don't know what you want from me. All I know is what my mother made me.*

Mater Lachrymarum leaned forward attentively, watching the girl with interest. *Show me,* she instructed.

Slowly, Justine turned to her mother. The two women looked at each other for a moment.

Then, Justine smiled; a hungry, vulpine grin that spread across her face like a stain, until it finally stretched into a rictus of incipient ferocity, a teeth-baring, animalistic snarl.

Justine's mother gazed at her daughter in horror. She could see nothing human remaining in those features, no discernible trace of the child she had borne and nurtured.

Transformed, the younger woman let out a vicious, guttural growl.

Her mother stumbled backwards, arms raised protectively. It was a hopeless gesture. Justine tore into her like a frenzied shark, her bloodlust irresistible, her teeth unerringly searching out the soft places on her mother's face and neck.

It went on for quite some time, the Three Mothers watching keenly for the entire duration of the attack.

When Justine was finally sated, she slumped backwards, completely spent. Her parent lay motionless beside her. Whatever family resemblance they once shared had been completely obliterated, reduced to an abstract bloody smear. Now, the older woman was nothing more than meat.

Slowly, Justine began to lick her mother's blood from her hands.

She heard a soft rustle of movement as the Three Mothers drew closer, forming a vigilant circle around her. Justine did not look up, her catlike tongue energetically bathing her fingers. Her mother had bled quite considerably.

Then, she heard three voices speaking in unison, speaking as one; and the single word they uttered was *daughter*.

The Devil

Telly Savalas in *Lisa e il diavolo*
(*Lisa and the Devil*), 1974
written by Mario Bava, Alfredo Leone, Giorgio Maulini
and Roberto Natale
directed by Mario Bava

They're bitches, Corso, the Devil said. *All of them, bitches.*

Dean Corso sat on the floor in the middle of the library, surrounded by teetering towers of books. He had spent his day – as he had spent *every* day since he had first arrived here – sorting the room's numerous bookshelves. The routine was always the same. The Devil would come in searching for a particular volume, and would invariably be unable to find it. He would then demand Corso reorganise the library's entire stock according to whatever new scheme He decided upon that day – by subject, perhaps, or alphabetically by author surname.

Corso was currently in the process of rearranging the books by the colour of their spines – an entirely useless endeavour made even more pointless by the knowledge that upon its completion, he would immediately have to begin the task all over again according to whatever new schema he was presented with.

He wanted to die.

Admittedly, he might *already* be dead. Corso honestly had no idea. He had no actual memory of dying, but had decided that the other denizens of the villa were almost certainly all long-deceased. A tedious mob of dissolute aristocrats, they wandered the rooms and corridors of the grand old building like laboratory rats, enacting the same morbid psychodramas time and time again. The one exception was a hot little blonde number, but she never seemed quite sure whether her name was Lisa or Elena, and Corso had eventually given up trying to get any sense out of her.

When he had first arrived at the house, Corso had done his best to fit in and dine with the others from time to time, but the pall of ennui that hung over the dinner table was such that he was soon seized by an irresistible urge to stab himself with the carving knife. Not only that, but on one occasion he'd glanced up from his soup to find the other diners had all somehow transformed into lifeless waxworks. Corso prided himself on being mostly unflappable, but that little stunt had entirely ruined his appetite.

Thereafter, he had restricted his movements almost entirely to the library. No one bothered him here, and at least the Sisyphean monotony of his labours was occasionally relieved by Leandro – as He insisted on being called here – bringing him whisky and cigarettes.

The villa's other residents all seemed entirely ignorant of the majordomo's true identity. When Corso had tried to convince them Leandro was, in fact, the Devil Himself, the assembled gentry had hooted with mirth. *We're all intellectuals here*, one of them had told him contemptuously. *We don't believe in such peasant nonsense.*

But the Devil He was, and He was all Corso had in the way of company. In His own manner, the Devil had taken something of a liking to Corso, and would regularly visit him in the library. There, they would both sit amongst the stacks of unshelved books, share a drink and a cigarette, and philosophise at length about whichever topic took their fancy.

Today, the subject was women.

Corso had been loudly bemoaning his

current predicament, a pastime that ranked a close third to smoking and drinking in terms of the time it generally occupied in his day-to-day existence. As far as he was concerned, the blame for the chain of diabolical events that had landed him in this damned villa could be laid squarely at the feet of the so-called fairer sex. In his experience, women were both wanton and viciously deceitful, a potently effective combination that Corso might have ruefully admired in an opponent had he not already fallen prey to it so many times already.

He might, however, have expected the Devil to appreciate such qualities, but was surprised to learn that the Prince of Darkness shared his views entirely. He, too, claimed to have ample cause to distrust the female of the species.

You see, Corso, the Devil began, *it was all so simple at first. Women were predictable creatures; weak and simple-minded and easy to manipulate. Take that whole business with Eve and the apple.*

I thought that was all just a story, said Corso. *Surely we're not meant to take that Garden of Eden shit literally.*

Literally, metaphorically, at heart the point is exactly the same. Women were put here to serve, to do precisely what men told them. You don't even have to take my word for it! It's all right there, in the Bible.

Corso had always maintained that quoting the Bible was the last refuge of a scoundrel, and here was the uncontestable proof of it. He diplomatically poured them both another whisky, while the Devil continued.

But they wised up. They figured out ways to flatter and beguile men and since then, it's all been one long race to the bottom. Take my son.

Corso's eyebrows raised. *You have a son?*

I disowned him, the miserable wretch.

The Devil let out a long, regretful sigh, his face etched with the kind of bitter disappointment only a parent can appreciate.

Earth was his for the taking. I gave him money, power, everything – and he fucked it all up. But do you know what happened? A woman literally stabbed him in the back. Some little whore he'd taken up the ass and then discarded. It's the same old story: a woman scorned. He let her get too close, and bang! Everything's ruined. All my plans for him, reduced to ashes. Do you know the lengths I had to go to? I even had to fuck a jackal, for Christ's sake. Some mangy, flea-bitten cur that tried to turn and bite me the whole time.

Corso thought that sounded like half the women he'd ever been to bed with. *I'm sorry,* he told the Devil, privately grateful that he'd never wanted children himself.

And that was only the start of it. Once he was safely out of the way, do you know who stepped in then?

No.

The Devil spat. *Those three witch bitches. Suspiriorum, Tenebrarum, and Lachrymarum. The Three Mothers.*

Corso sat up in his seat, remembering the book of the same name he'd so fatefully failed to acquire. *What happened?*

What always *happens? They let a man do all the hard work, then thought they could sneak in and take it all for themselves afterwards. That's how equality works, am I right? I gave my son the entire world to play with, and when he went and dropped the ball, they snatched it away for themselves. I wouldn't even be surprised if that cunt who stabbed him worked for them. It sounds exactly like their style.*

The Devil gestured for Corso to pass him the cigarettes. Removing one from the packet, He ignited its tip with a mere flick of his fingers. It was a piece of casual showmanship that never failed to impress Corso.

Have you met them? Corso asked, after his companion had taken a few ruminative pulls of tobacco.

Oh, of course. I always make sure to meet every witch personally, you know. It's part of the whole deal.

The old infernal casting couch routine, eh? Corso said wryly.

The Devil looked momentarily haughty. *Look, Corso, don't think for a moment they didn't all want it. I haven't met a woman yet who doesn't go damp at the crotch at the first sniff of real power. Those three bitches may claim now that what happened wasn't consensual, but believe me, they knew what they were getting into. They all made a choice, and they benefited from it.*

Corso said nothing. God knows his own track record with women wasn't entirely spotless, but even he drew the line somewhere. Confidence tricks were one thing, but he'd learned the hard way that short-sighted men in glasses were temperamentally unsuited to any form of violence, be it sexual or otherwise. Besides, as a rare book dealer in New York City, he'd come across more than one moneyed predator over the course of his career, and they never failed to turn his stomach. You could always bet that they'd carry over whatever vile little habits they'd learned in the bedroom to the rest of their day-to-day existence; accordingly, Corso had made it a general rule in life to fuck them first whenever possible.

Oblivious to his companion's silence, the Devil continued with his tirade. He got to his feet and angrily kicked over a stack of books, then turned to glower at Corso. *I mean, have you even seen what half of these women look like? It's no accident they ended up as unmarried spinsters living alone in the woods, let me tell you! Hooked noses, warts, tits down to their knees – all of the clichés are true! And I was the poor bastard that was meant to show them a good time! Do you really think I enjoyed that?*

The dealer waved his hands placatingly. *I know, I know...*

The Devil's face had grown ruddy with anger, and Corso could have sworn that the helices of His ears were slowly growing more pointed. *Look, I'm used to you little people trying to wriggle out of the deals you make with me. It gets tiresome after a while, but I understand, it's all a part of the game. But don't waste my precious time summoning me up for a night of passion and then pretend it wasn't exactly what you wanted afterwards. It's like the actress going up to the producer's hotel suite and then claiming she thought she was just there for an audition, you know?*

Corso clambered up from the couch and began to pull at his necktie. It was becoming oppressively stuffy in the room. *Well, I should really get back to work...*

His companion dropped his cigarette to the floor and ground it out with his heel. *Forgive me, Corso. Talking about those three makes me...intemperate. But I'm going to put an end to it all, I assure you. They're going to regret ever uttering my name.*

He strode from the room, slamming the door behind him. Corso exhaled in relief, slumping back against a nearby bookcase. As much as he'd come to appreciate the occasional diversions offered by the Devil's company, he was glad that particular conversation had come to an end. Better to stick to less emotive topics in future, the dealer decided. He did not wish to risk offending his malefic captor, for fear of earning himself a far worse punishment than merely being banished to this goddamned library.

Christ, it was hot in here. It felt as though the

smallest spark would be enough to send the whole library up in flames.

Corso decided he would take a short stroll around the grounds. It would be cool outside in the night air – it was *always* nighttime in the villa – and perhaps the lingering after-effects of the Devil's rage would have dissipated by the time he returned.

The villa was situated deep in the woods, and Corso decided to walk along the periphery of the trees for a ways, where he was confident he would not bump into any of the house's other inhabitants. Everyone else avoided the dark forest, for fear of getting lost and never being able to find their way back. By now, they were all well-accustomed to the creature comforts offered by their own peculiar form of damnation, and the thought of any other kind of Hell was quite intolerable.

Enjoying the feel of the evening breeze on his skin, Corso paused to light yet another cigarette. If there was a single upside to his fate, he mused, it was that he imagined he was unlikely to develop cancer in whatever limbo this was that he found himself consigned to. Although he was always exceedingly careful to keep such thoughts to himself, lest he give the Devil any bright ideas.

As he relished the asperous bliss of cigarette smoke entering his lungs, he was distracted by a sudden noise – the sound of approaching feet crashing through the forest undergrowth nearby. He immediately froze. Who – or what – could possibly be emerging from the depths of that boundless black abyss?

Given the choice of fight or flight, Corso would normally opt for the latter every time, but as he readied himself to flee, a shaft of moonlight pierced the canopy of trees and revealed the oncoming figure to be a young woman – slender, small in stature, posing no obvious threat. Intrigued, Corso decided to remain where he was and took another steadying drag of tobacco while he waited for her to reach him.

The woman exited the treeline and looked at Corso with trepidation. *Please...can you help me?*

Her accent was American. She was thin and pale, with black hair and wide surprised eyes that seemed almost too large for her face. Something about her put Corso in mind of a heroine from a fairytale.

I'm not sure, he replied. *But I can try.*

You're American? She sounded surprised.

Well, I certainly used to be, he mused.

So where am I?

I'm not entirely sure of that either, said Corso apologetically. *Where do you think you are?*

A few hours ago, I was in the Black Forest, in Germany, the young woman said.

Corso looked back at the villa. *Well, wherever this is, I'm pretty sure it isn't Germany.*

I don't understand! the young woman wailed. *I got away! I killed her, but the Academy was burning...everything was falling apart, so I ran out into the forest, and...*

Killed? Before Corso could interrogate her further, her eyelids began to flutter, and she stumbled forwards in a swoon. He managed to catch her before she crumpled to the ground. Her delicate frame weighed no more than one of the bizarre dummies Leandro was forever carrying around the villa.

Corso lowered her carefully to the grass. After a few moments, she opened her eyes and looked weakly up at him. *I'm sorry, I...*

The young woman made to try and rise, but Corso gently restrained her. *Rest for a moment,* he told her. *You've had a shock.*

She accepted this without complaint.

Maybe you should tell me your name, Corso said. *Mine's Corso.*

I'm Suzy, she said. *Suzy Bannion.*

So tell me about the Black Forest, Suzy, he said.

I was studying ballet there. At the Tanz Akademie. I was so happy at first! But it was an awful place. The teachers and staff were really strange, and my friends kept, well, disappearing. And you won't believe this, but...

Her voice dropped to a whisper. *It turned out they were witches, all of them.*

Witches? Suddenly Suzy's mysterious arrival at the villa seemed less than purely coincidental.

I know, it's crazy.

Maybe not. What else?

The leader of the coven was named Helena Markos. They called her the Black Queen. She lived in a secret part of the building, but I found my way in there, and...and...

Tears glistened in her eyes. Corso took her hand. *You don't have to tell me if you don't want to,* he said.

No, I want to. If I tell you I might even be able to believe it myself. I went into her room, and I could hear her voice – god, it was horrible, all scratchy and old, like a storybook witch, you know? But I couldn't see her! She was invisible! And then my friend Sara was there, but she was dead, and she had needles stuck in her eyes, and she was trying to kill me!

This was all getting pretty far-fetched, even by Corso's recent standards.

Suzy went on. *I know how it sounds, but it's the truth, I swear. I thought I was going to die in there. But there was a storm outside, you see, and when the lightning flashed, I could see her. Just her shape, like someone had drawn a line around her. It was enough, though. I stabbed her in her neck, and then I could see her properly, and it almost made me sick to look at her, she was so ugly, and old, and...*

What happened then?

I just ran. The building was falling apart around my ears, so I ran as fast as I could. Right out into the forest. But then it was so dark, and cold, and eventually I just couldn't run any more. I lay down under a tree and passed out, I think. And then I had a dream, only it was so vivid, it was like it was really happening...

Corso fumbled for another cigarette. He offered Suzy the pack, but she declined. Once his cigarette was lit, she continued with her story.

I dreamt there were other people with me in the

forest. Two women. One of them was very beautiful, but kinda scary too. And I couldn't really see the other one, she kept to the shadows. Then the beautiful one spoke to me. 'Child,' she said. 'You have caused great harm to our sister.'

Sister?

That's what she said, I guess Helena Markos was their sister? Although it seemed like she was much, much older than the other two.

Three sisters. Three witches. Corso took a lungful of smoke and silently considered what this new piece of information could possibly mean.

And then she told me, 'You are brave, and pure of heart, and we applaud your courage. But you are an unruly, mischievous child, breaking things that are old and priceless beyond your imagining, and there must be a reckoning.'

After that, the other one whispered, 'Send her to His house and let her continue her games there.'

And her sister laughed and said, 'The Morningstar? Ah sister, as always, your cruelty is unmatched.'

Well, I didn't know what any of that meant, and I was getting scared – she had these really freaky blue eyes that made you feel like you were underwater, drowning – so I got up and ran. And then I saw a light in the distance, so I headed for it, and then you were standing there, and now I don't know where I am!

Suzy dissolved into tears. Corso did his best to comfort her, but empathy had never been his strong suit. So instead, he told her, *Let's get you inside. A drink would probably do you good.*

Privately, he didn't like to think about what might happen once the Devil discovered Suzy had been sent here by the Three Mothers, but after a lifetime spent thinking on his feet, Corso was willing to try and traverse that particular bridge when he came to it.

He escorted her inside the villa and into the library, where she gratefully drooped down onto the leather sofa. He then proceeded to fetch her a tumbler of whisky, at which Suzy pulled a disgusted face. Still, Corso insisted, and so she reluctantly swallowed the fiery liquid, grimacing emphatically as she did so, like a small child forced to take their medicine.

Hurriedly wiping the taste from her lips, Suzy gazed around the library with increasing wonder. *Are all these your books?*

Corso scowled, saying nothing. Then, a sudden thought struck him.

What year is it out there? he asked Suzy. It had been 1999 when he first came here, but time had little or no meaning in the villa, and Corso found he desperately wanted to know how many months – or even years – had passed in the real world. Not that it would amount to much, given the apparently indefinite nature of his sentence.

She looked at him curiously. *It's 1977, of course.*

1977! The library began to lurch and sway around Corso, like a room in a funhouse. He stumbled over to the couch and collapsed beside Suzy, the ancient sofa letting out a defeated sigh that echoed Corso's own overwhelming despair.

Oh, Christ, he moaned. *Then it really is hopeless. I'm trapped here forever, completely unstuck in time.*

Suzy took his hand consolingly. *I don't understand. Why can't you just leave?*

It may not look like it, but this place is a prison. There's no way out. The people here, we're all damned.

It's just a big old house. You could walk out anytime you liked.

You don't understand, Suzy...

A look of impish glee crept over her doll-like features. *I thought I was trapped in a bad house too. But do you know what I did? I just burnt it down.*

Corso looked terrified at the very thought of it. *No, I couldn't...*

She giggled. *I bet I could.*

Without waiting for permission, Suzy slipped her hand into Corso's jacket pocket and removed his box of matches with a grin. *All these books. All this paper.*

Suzy! If He catches you...

She jumped to her feet and nimbly began to dance between the stacks of books. *Who's He? I just killed a big bad witch, I'm not scared!* She pirouetted towards Corso's desk, snatching up his whisky decanter in one hand.

Suzy, please! Corso wanted to get up, to stop her before it was too late, but all strength had fled from his legs.

She laughed, upending the decanter over a nearby pile of books and drenching them in whisky. Then she deftly struck a match, holding it poised over the topmost volume on the stack, an impossibly rare first edition of *Paradise Lost*.

Shall I?

Despite the unspeakable terror that gripped him, Corso suddenly realised he very much wanted to see the book burn. To watch the whole damn lot of them blacken and shrivel away to nothing.

But before he could reply to Suzy, an enraged voice boomed out from the library entrance. *CORSO!*

Corso looked around to see his jailer standing in the doorway, his eyes flaming embers. The Devil pointed a long, accusing finger at Suzy, its nail slowly warping into a curled yellow talon. *Who is she?* He demanded.

The book dealer was dimly aware of his bladder letting go, although the warmth in his crotch at least provided some respite from the deathly chill that was rapidly spreading throughout the rest of his body.

The match Suzy held in her outstretched hand was close to burning down completely. So, rather than sear her fingers, she simply dropped it.

Oops, she said.

The books ignited into bright orange flame.

NO! the Devil screamed, rushing forward into the room, arms outstretched like a swooping bird of prey. He seemed to be lunging directly at Suzy, but when she skipped gracefully aside, he ignored her and threw himself headlong into the burning tower of books, in a desperate attempt to smother the proliferating flames with the weight of his body.

Too late. Such was the chaotic proximity of the piled stacks of books that the fire had quickly spread in all directions. In mere seconds, the blaze had become unstoppable; a rampant, roaring beast that could not be contained.

Corso stared around him. He'd never witnessed anything quite so beautiful; an untrammeled inferno of knowledge and reason. He only wished he had a drink left in his glass to toast the destruction of his own private Hell.

Suddenly, Suzy appeared before him. *Come on!* she cried, seizing his arm and pulling him to his feet. Faced with the option of remaining where he was and burning alive, Corso discovered that he could muster the strength to stand after all.

His rescuer dragged him towards the library doorway, rushing to get to safety before the flames cut them off.

Another shriek of rage prompted Corso to glance back over his shoulder. He could not gaze for too long at the burning room, so intense was the heat thrown off by the rapidly-swelling furnace, but thought he glimpsed a winged figure, vaguely reptilian in outline, stumbling through the capering flames, like a drunk intruding on a ballroom dancefloor.

Once they had reached the sanctuary of the garden, they fell gratefully onto the lawn. Lying there gasping like a fish, Corso could hear the alarmed cries of the villa's other inhabitants in the distance. He had no idea what would happen to them all once the building burnt to the ground, and could not honestly say he gave a damn.

Suzy looked at him and giggled, her eyes large and bright. *That was fun*, she said.

Corso was forced to admit that it had been, after a fashion. He looked over at Suzy in wonderment. On the face of it, she seemed so helpless and frail, and yet she'd somehow survived encounters with the Mother of Sighs and the Devil Himself.

Perhaps it was high time to reconsider his position on women.

But what now? He stared over at the impenetrable black wall of trees that surrounded the villa. *I don't know where we go from here*, he told Suzy. His momentary elation at having escaped the library was swiftly dimming.

Brushing ash from her dress, Suzy got to her feet and extended a delicate hand to Corso. *Come on,* she told him briskly. *No sense in waiting around here, anyway.*

Her sense of abandon was becoming infectious. Taking her hand, he allowed her to pull him upright and lead him towards the forest. *But what if we get lost in there?* he said.

She smiled. *I'm sure we'll find a trail of breadcrumbs to lead us home,* she replied.

Hand in hand, they disappeared into the trees.

The Woman

Béatrice Dalle in *À l'intérieur*
(Inside), 2007
written & directed by
Alexandre Bustillo and Julien Maury

She'd possessed a name once, she was sure of it.

Sometimes, in her dreams, she could almost remember the woman she had been. She would recall images, puzzle fragments of a forgotten life – a handsome young lover, a beach house, a lost child – and at those times, her sleeping mind could sense that the truth about herself was practically within reach. Her tongue would begin to curl, ready to utter her own name aloud like a spell, just two simple syllables; the magical key that would unlock everything. She knew that if she could only force herself awake, she would surface from dream with the word poised on her lips, a sunken treasure rescued from the black depths of sleep.

But she never could. It were as though she were a blind woman, desperately flailing to catch a solitary feather drifting on the breeze. She would fumble and paw at the air, and occasionally feel the momentary touch of the feather's barbs on her fingertips; but by the time she could react, it would have danced out of reach once more.

Inevitably, such dreams would instead end with a soft, suffocating whiteness descending upon her like a fog. It would press down on her face, expunging all life from her body, and with it, her thoughts and memories, everything that had made her the person she once was. She would awake gasping for breath, clawing frantically at her face, and by the time she had recovered from the nightmare, the name would be gone, with only the faintest sweet aftertaste of it lingering on her tongue. The suggestion of it in her mouth would then distress her so much that she would down several shots of cold vodka in an attempt to wash the sensation away.

It was far better not to know, she tried to tell herself. All she was now, all she would ever be, belonged to Mater Tenebrarum. Any traces of her past life had been completely eradicated, cleansed by her unholy baptism. She had been summoned back from the bright light which had claimed her and thrust into the shadow-haunted domain of the Mother of Darkness.

Her only purpose now was to serve.

When the Woman first entered her matriarch's service, it was during a period of upheaval. Mater Tenebrarum's great old house in New York had been razed in a terrible fire, and consequently she had returned to Europe and taken up residence with her sister Mater Lachrymarum in Rome. The occasion constituted something of a family reunion, as their elder sibling Mater Suspiriorum also now inhabited the same building, although not in a strictly physical sense; her own home and body having been destroyed some years before in Germany.

Thus reunited, the Three Mothers focused on consolidating their power, recruiting more acolytes to their ranks of followers, and preparing for the war they knew would inevitably arrive. The Woman was one such acolyte amongst many, a deadly drone with no name and but one purpose; to protect and serve her dark queen.

Nevertheless, she managed to distinguish herself in those early days. Despite her rebirth into Mater Tenebrarum's service, she still possessed a nascent streak of madness and violence, a remnant of her previous existence imprinted so deeply within her that even the Mother's sorcery could not wipe it away. Indeed, once her mistress recognised its presence, she eagerly nurtured and encouraged it, enabling her new servant to quickly flourish and grow into one of the Mother's most trusted assassins. She became adept at killing and magic both, murdering scores of enemies during her subsequent decades of service. If anything, her only flaw was the sheer glee she took in butchery; a simple kill alone would never suffice. Instead, she would not stop until the walls were red with her victim's blood, as though each individual drop constituted another offering to her matriarch.

However, as the years went on, the dreams continued, and with them, a growing sense of lack, of absence. She became gripped by the idea that she'd once had a child, which had somehow become lost to her, and the gnawing emptiness she felt quickly became an all-consuming obsession. Fearful of the consequences should the Mother of Darkness learn of her doubts, the Woman therefore said nothing of the phantom child she mourned, protecting her secret like a flame cupped between her hands, waiting for the time when it burned bright and strong enough to be set free.

In the early years of the new millennium, the Woman was summoned to Mater Tenebrarum's presence. She entered the darkened sanctum and knelt down in supplication, waiting for her mistress to speak.

A voice rasped from the shadows. It reminded the Woman of a poisonous insect scuttling across the ground, its chitinous underbelly scraping over stone.

There is a man, in Rome. His name is Mark Elliot. He alone escaped the destruction of my home in New York. His continued existence is an affront to me.

There was more, but the Woman barely heard it. All she ever needed was a name. The reason was not hers to question.

It did not take her long to locate Elliot. Forever changed by his encounter with the Mother of Darkness, he had returned to Rome a shattered and fearful man. A veil had been torn from his eyes, and finding himself incapable of confronting the horror of what he now beheld, Elliot had instead sought refuge in drugs and alcohol. A once-promising musical career soon came to naught, and now he eked out a living playing piano in cocktail bars; that is, when he wasn't too drunk or stoned to perform. It was obvious to all who knew him that the slightest nudge would send him sprawling into the gutter forever.

In truth, the Woman barely saw the point of taking Elliot's life. He had no real friends to speak of, and the lowlife rabble he did associate with laughed and rolled their eyes whenever Elliot began to mutter darkly about the malevolent forces that surrounded them all. To them, he was just another crackpot junkie paranoid, given to incoherent rants about entirely imaginary threats. They gave no more credence to Elliot's crazed stories of the Three Mothers than they would to theories of the Illuminati or black helicopters.

The Woman trailed Elliot for a week, drifting behind him from dive bar to dive bar, as unobtrusive as the man's own shadow. She had any number of opportunities to kill him, but something stayed her hand. In some inexplicable manner, Elliot reminded her of someone. As the Woman followed him across the city, so in turn was she hounded by another dark spectre; albeit one that only existed in the furthest recesses of her own mind.

And whenever she lay down to sleep at night, the dreams returned. Dreams of another man, another dissolute artist; one she had loved to the point of insanity. She dreamt of the sea, and of blood, and always, finally, of that awful smothering whiteness.

At last she could bear it no more. She decided that carrying out her duty was the only way to put an end to the delusions that freshly tormented her. She would enact Mater Tenebrarum's vengeance, wipe this broken, pitiful man from the face of the earth, and with him her own tortured fantasies.

That night, she emerged from the shadows in the corner of his squalid room, to find Elliot wide awake, nursing a bottle and anticipating her arrival.

Masking her surprise, she slowly approached the bed where he lay.

I've been hoping you'd come, he said. *I've seen you following me.*

Then you know who I am, and why I'm here, she replied.

Yes. He paused, his red-rimmed eyes studying her. *You're very beautiful.*

She did not think of herself in such a manner, not anymore, and it stopped her for a moment.

Am I?

He laughed sourly. *Undoubtedly. Mind you, I think I've been in love with death ever since that night I saw Her. I've spent the rest of my miserable life trying to find Her again.*

And now She has found you.

Elliot took a long pull from the bottle, then asked her: *Am I permitted a last request?*

The Woman said nothing, waiting for him to summon the courage to make it. In time, he did, although there was an audible tremor in his voice when he spoke.

Would you lie with me a while?

The Woman considered this. She thought of the fantasies that assailed her at night, and of that long-lost lover in the shack by the sea. And she decided.

Stepping out of her black cloak and dress, she climbed naked into bed with the man. They made for clumsy, awkward lovers: him, out of practice and dull with drink; her, a virgin made anew, shy and inexperienced. Still, they were both gentle, and enjoyed each other for the short time they were allotted, and when she finally reached down besides the bed, picked up her blade and cut his throat, she did it quickly and cleanly, so that he might not suffer.

As she dressed afterwards, her hand moved to her abdomen. Yes, she was sure of it. She could feel the soft heat building inside her already.

She would bear the man's child, and replace that which she had lost.

Not knowing what else to do, she ran. She had no doubt that the Mother of Darkness would severely punish such a transgression, so she stole a car and set out on the road, living from day-to-day, week-to-week, always watchful, always wary.

The Three Mothers had eyes everywhere.

She changed vehicles frequently, and never stayed in any one place too long. Initially she headed west, travelling down through Croatia and Albania into Greece, and then back up again through Macedonia and Serbia, marking the passing days by the gradual swelling of her belly.

Her plan was to have the child in France, where, from what little she could ascertain about her past life, she herself had originally been born. Secretly, the Woman doubted whether she would ever succeed in making it that far, but as the months slowly passed and she grew heavier with child, a small part of her began to hope against all hope that, in exchange for her years of loyal service, Mater Tenebrarum had granted her this small mercy; all this despite the fact that benevolence was not a quality she would have hitherto ascribed to the Mother of Darkness.

And yet, when disaster did finally strike her, it owed nothing to the machinations of the Three Mothers and everything to random misfortune. The Woman had finally reached France, where she had rented a small accommodation and made private arrangements to have her baby at home. She was determined that absolutely nothing should go wrong with the pregnancy. One life had been stripped from her already; she would fight tooth and nail to preserve the meagre scraps of the one she had now.

So when the car accident killed her unborn child, mere days before she was due to give birth, the Woman's rage and grief knew no bounds.

The insanity buried at the core of her being, the long-suppressed madness previously kept in check by her Mother's indomitable influence, was finally unleashed. At first she was certain that the fatal collision must have been the work of her erstwhile matriarch, but it soon became apparent that it was nothing more than simple bad luck. Recuperating in the hospital afterwards, the Woman read in the newspaper that a male passenger in the other car had also been killed, although his wife, who had been driving and was the only other occupant of the vehicle, had survived with relatively minor injuries. She was, in fact, being kept in the very same hospital.

The Woman's first thought was to track her down and slaughter her where she lay. But when she read the next line of the report, everything else was forgotten.

The widowed woman, one Sarah Scarangella, had not only lived, but was also pregnant.

A cruel joke, worthy in its unmitigated malignity of Mater Tenebrarum herself. If the Mother had planned it this way, the Woman's punishment could not be any more fitting. She did not know whether to laugh or scream.

And yet...there was a certain symmetry to it. Sarah Scarangella had to pay for the unborn life she had taken, that much was clear. But why simply murder her when it would be far more apposite for the Woman to wait until Sarah's own child was due – and then simply seize it for her own? Rendering her desolate and alone, just like the Woman herself.

The Woman fled the hospital that night, but she did not go far. A few days later, when Sarah was discharged from care, the Woman was there, watching. She proceeded to follow Sarah home, and continued to observe her prey as the newly-widowed woman entered the house she had shared with her deceased husband. The tears came quickly, and Sarah's unseen stalker relished each and every one of them.

She maintained her observation of Sarah over the coming months, her hatred growing in tandem with the pregnant woman's child. In that sense, the two women proceeded in lockstep, each nurturing something inside themselves; one preparing to usher new life into the world; the other readying herself to deliver only violence and death.

It was Christmas Eve when the Woman

finally struck. Sarah was scheduled to give birth the next day, and, perhaps unable to stomach the mawkish symbolism of the assigned due date, her watcher found she could delay no longer. She attempted to gain entry to the house via deceptive means, and when a suspicious Sarah refused her entry, the Woman was forced to resort to the magicks taught to her by the Mother of Darkness, something she had resisted doing until now for fear of attracting Mater Tenebrarum's attention.

She materialised inside the house and quickly attacked, but failed in her first attempt to kill the sleeping Sarah. It should have been a trivial matter for such a practiced assassin, but the Woman's quarry proved unexpectedly resourceful, and as vicious as a cornered lioness in her maternal instincts. By the time the bloodshed came to an end, Sarah's home had been transformed into a slaughterhouse. Six people lay butchered, and Sarah herself was soon to join their number. Fatally injured, she begged her attacker to save the life of her child. The Woman, grievously wounded herself, calmly cut the pregnant woman open and safely delivered her baby girl, leaving Sarah to bleed to death.

Bloodied and burned almost beyond recognition, the Woman took the newborn she had claimed as her own and collapsed into a chair. Ignoring the shrieking pain that coursed through her body, she rocked the crying child in her arms, calming its post-natal anxiety.

As she sat there, she slowly became aware of another presence in the room, something gathering itself in the darkness, much as she herself had done only an hour or so before.

Mother, she breathed.

A familiar voice hissed from the shadows. *You are no longer my daughter.*

When the hot tears sprang to the Woman's eyes, she did not know what to make of them. She had never before wept, not in this new life, and she could not comprehend whether she was crying at Mater Tenebrarum's rejection, or at the surety that the motherhood she had desperately craved for so long was about to be ripped away from her once more.

So, overwhelmed by the strange unfamiliarity of her grief, she simply sobbed like a infant; incoherently, wordlessly.

Mater Tenebrarum silently observed her misery for a few moments, then spoke again.

I should kill you now.

Please...

The Woman's voice died in her throat, like a budding flower in a spring frost. She knew it was useless to beg.

But I think perhaps it will be crueller to let you live.

Mother...?

The Woman looked around, bewildered. She was alone in the room once more.

She did not understand what Mater Tenebrarum had meant, or why she had spared her, but there would be time enough to worry about that later. For now, she had to get her daughter out of here before the authorities arrived. Taking Sarah's car, she stole away into the night.

Her injuries would have proven fatal for any mortal human, but when she had been reborn into the Three Mothers' service, the Woman had been gifted with supernaturally-increased powers of stamina and recuperation. Even so, it took her many days to recover from her wounds, and the beauty Mark Elliot had remarked upon would be forever disfigured.

Still, she cared little for that now. She had regained the love she thought had been lost to her forever, and with it, perhaps, a small piece of the person she once was.

The Woman escaped deep into the French countryside, where she raised her infant daughter in seclusion. She named the baby Lisa – the name seemed to have some unknown resonance for her – and they lived in perfect happiness together for the first few years of the young girl's life. The Woman often thought of Mater Tenebrarum's last words to her, and pondered their possible implications. Accordingly, she feared some terrible harm coming to Lisa, and made sure to keep her close at all times.

So, when the child eventually began to approach school age, the Woman dreaded the prospect of being separated from her, fearful of what might befall Lisa without her mother there to protect her. Still, she knew she could not deny her daughter an education, determined as she was that Lisa should have all of the opportunities any normal girl would enjoy, opportunities that had been forever denied to her adoptive mother. Reluctantly, she enrolled the girl in the local school, and when the time came for her to begin her classes, the Woman cried for only the second time that she could remember.

Lisa was an outgoing, happy child, and immediately took to school and her classmates, so much so that she began to grow impatient at being kept inside the rest of the time. *I want to go out and play*, she would whine to her mother, who habitually avoided the outside world whenever she could. But despite her persistent fears, there was very little that the Woman could ever refuse her daughter, and so, one afternoon, she agreed to accompany Lisa on an expedition to the local playground, where a number of Lisa's schoolfriends would be gathered to play.

Donning the black veil she always wore on her infrequent sojourns outdoors, the Woman walked Lisa to the playground, then took a seat on a nearby bench and watched as her daughter played happily with the other children. Really, what harm could befall her here? The day was warm and bright, their surroundings alive with the scents and colours of springtime. Despite the Woman's instinctive wariness, the local people had been nothing but welcoming to her and Lisa. Even in a poisoned world where the hidden rot of the Three Mothers was never very far from the surface, this seemed to be a safe place, a refuge.

So when the Woman noticed the new girl joining in with the rest of the children's games, she thought nothing of it at first. She had never seen the child before, and was immediately struck by her almost-angelic beauty. The girl was a few years older than the other children, and so quickly began to take charge, taking each of them aside in turn and whispering into their ear. When the girl reached Lisa, the younger child listened intently to her instructions, then looked over at her mother and laughed.

Before long, the assembled children gathered themselves together in a tight huddle, their newfound angel at their centre, murmuring secrets. The Woman grew unaccountably disturbed. The sight of the children clustered together put her in mind of a conspiracy; the sort of unhallowed congregation she herself had once belonged to.

She got to her feet and began to approach the children, calling out to Lisa as she went. *Lisa, time we went home now! You can play again another day!*

As she drew closer, the ranks of the children parted, revealing the older girl. Seeing the Woman, the girl smiled and waved.

Hello, Betty, she said. Her smile widened insinuatingly. *That is your name, isn't it?*

The Woman immediately stumbled to a halt, as though she had just walked into an invisible barrier. She stared at the girl in horrified fascination.

Betty.

The name she had tried to recall for so long, the key that had always slipped from her sleeping fingers. The girl was right. She *was* Betty, she realised.

That one revelation was like a tiny crack in the glass wall of an aquarium; it rapidly widened and shattered, letting forth a deluge of suppressed memories, drowning her with their cumulative, unrelenting power.

Betty sank to her knees, helpless. Now, finally, she remembered everything.

The life she had lived as a young woman, the man she had loved beyond all reason. The irrevocable insanity that had claimed her. And her death at her lover's hands, as he thrust a heavy pillow over her face to forever shut out the world that had driven her into the depths of madness.

Betty let out a mournful howl, a she-wolf

trapped in a hunter's snare. She only wished that Mater Tenebrarum had taken her life when she had the opportunity, and now, at last, understood why she hadn't.

She gazed up at the girl, whose eyes suddenly seemed ineffably, wickedly, ancient.

Tell those three bitches I'm coming for them, croaked the girl.

She then motioned the other children forward. Betty noticed that their small hands now all clutched makeshift weapons; rocks, branches, whatever they'd been able to scavenge from the wooded perimeter of the playground.

Lisa stood with them, a piece of broken glass glinting in her hand.

You can play with her now, the Devil told them.

And when they fell upon her, Betty almost welcomed it.

Francesco Dellamorte

Rupert Everett in *Dellamorte Dellamore*
(Cemetery Man), 1994
written by Gianni Romoli
based on the novel by Tiziano Sclavi
directed by Michele Soavi

Francesco Dellamorte awoke from a dream of dying to find himself lying alone on a desolate grey beach. Struggling up onto his elbows, he stared out at the incoming tide, the waves crashing against the shoreline with a sound like shattering glass.

Where *was* he? And where was his faithful assistant Gnaghi? True, the man was a congenital idiot, but at least you always knew where you were with an idiot. Gnaghi was devoted and loyal, and that was not something Dellamorte could say about anyone else in his life. Certainly not the many women he had loved.

(Or was it only one? He couldn't quite recall.)

But now Gnaghi was gone. Dellamorte's habitual melancholy suddenly threatened to overwhelm him. A hermit by temperament, he found himself seized by an entirely unfamiliar sensation: a devastating feeling of loneliness. It gripped him like a virus, sending a numb chill flooding through his body. His mind reeled. Sitting alone on the sand, he could not rid himself of the senseless notion that he might be the last man on Earth.

If, indeed, this *was* Earth.

Somehow, he had to get out of this terrible place and find Gnaghi, find *anybody*. Dellamorte got to his feet and gazed around at the surrounding landscape. The beach appeared to stretch on forever, a blasted panorama of eternal winter. At that moment, it seemed plausible that he might be doomed to walk it in perpetuity, struggling on and on across the infinite vista of wet sand, a lost sinner marooned in an endless Beckettian hell.

Then, he glimpsed the smallest of movements further up the shoreline. Squinting into the distance, he thought he could make out two figures hunched over a rock. Right now, it did not matter in the least to Dellamorte who they were or exactly what they were doing there; all he cared about was the fact that they promised some relief from this awful solitude. He immediately broke into a run.

As he drew closer, he could see the pair in more detail. They were deeply absorbed in a game of chess, the chessboard perched on the rock between them. One was a blond man with Scandinavian features, who appeared to be dressed in the uniform of a medieval knight.

The other player was dressed only in a black hooded cloak.

Dellamorte recognised the figure immediately, and felt an irrational spasm of morbid joy. Death had been his constant companion for many years now, and although they existed in a oscillating state of mutual antagonism, he was nevertheless relieved to see a familiar face.

Of course, what Francesco Dellamorte could never quite admit to himself was that he was deeply, irrationally, in love with Death.

When he finally reached the two chess players, the knight looked up to greet him, seeming to take some solace in Dellamorte's unexpected arrival.

Hail, good fellow, he said. *Would you like to challenge my companion to a game? I fear she has my measure, but perhaps fortune might smile more favourably upon you.*

I fucking hate chess, Dellamorte said, drawing his revolver and shooting the knight in the face.

The hooded figure gazed impassively down at the knight's fallen body. Dellamorte glimpsed the ivory gleam of bone in the recesses of its dark cowl.

She? So you're a woman now? he asked the figure, a little confused.

Perhaps I always was, the figure said in a female voice, thick with winter frost.

That puts a slightly different complexion on things, said Dellamorte.

How so?

Because I wanted to kill you, and keep on killing you, but now I think I might have to fuck you first.

The figure gave a low chuckle. *Perhaps I might even allow it, Dellamorte. That is, if you can find me first.*

And how do I do that?

I'll leave you a trail. Let's see if you're man enough to follow it.

Another game? Dellamorte said impatiently.

The figure gestured at the chessboard. *You would prefer chess?*

I'm not sure I trust you.

The figure sighed. *Oh, Dellamorte, Dellamorte,*

it scolded. *Name one solitary thing that is more certain in life, more reliable, than death?*

For now, grant me one kiss, then, said Dellamorte.

He moved closer, making to embrace the figure, until it seized one of his wrists in its bony grip, holding him at bay.

Not yet, lover.

A terrible, searing cold immediately flooded Dellamorte's senses, causing him to gasp.

Look for the Black Spider, his intended hissed.

At that moment, a huge wave swept in, engulfing everything and knocking Dellamorte to the ground. His lungs filled with seawater, and he thought for an instant that perhaps Death had cheated him after all.

When the tide finally subsided, he looked up, coughing and wiping the brine from his eyes. The hooded figure had vanished, leaving only the corpse of the knight behind, bobbing stiffly in the ocean like an oversized version of the chess pieces that now lay scattered in the sand.

Fine, said Dellamorte. *If you want to play it that way.*

He got back to his feet, brushing the wave's residue from his clothes. When he looked back towards the land, he could now glimpse an overgrown path leading up and away from the beach. If he were going to have to locate Death's trail, this seemed like as good a place as any to start.

The reference to the Black Spider eventually led him to a cursed Etruscan crypt near Rome, overrun with hordes of the returned. The whole area stank of death, the air thick with an almost tangible reek of corruption, and had been shunned by the local populace for decades. But the slow-moving dead, rendered stupid by the vicissitudes of the grave, offered no more of an obstacle to Dellamorte than had their counterparts in his home town of Buffalora.

As he stood watching a pile of inert corpses burn, a plume of fetid ash spiralling into the sky, Dellamorte sighed with a terrible ennui. *How long must we play this damn stupid game?* he shouted into the heavens.

In reply, the pall of smoke hanging above began to swirl and shift, as though it were being shaped by an unseen hand. As Dellamorte looked on, the cloud momentarily formed itself into a single letter: 'K'.

And exactly what the fuck is that meant to mean?

he muttered in exasperation, already tired of his opponent's schemes.

But there was nothing else for it. Death's was the only game in town.

Dellamorte proceeded to roam blindly across northern Italy for the next few weeks, until he finally learned of a scientist named Zeder, who had made the study of undeath his life's work. The man had identified a phenomena he called 'K-Zones', areas of land possessing the preternatural ability to resurrect the dead. There was a lot more bullshit scientific jargon involved, but quite frankly, Dellamorte didn't care. The dead had a nasty habit of coming back to life; he already understood that fact only too well. He paid as little heed to the reasons behind it as he did to understanding exactly why it rained. It was a damned inconvenience, that was the beginning and end of the matter. If there was a storm outside, you put on a raincoat, and if the dead returned, you shot them in the head.

The trail took him to a stretch of industrial wasteland outside Bologna, where the site of a long-abandoned building had been supposedly earmarked for redevelopment into a luxury hotel. Dellamorte found the derelict building sealed off, but there was no evidence of any actual construction work being carried out. The whole thing was just a cover story to keep out prying eyes. Forcing his way inside, he discovered a field laboratory had been set up on the premises to document the uncanny properties of the K-Zone that had been discovered in the area. To this end, a single laboratory worker sat watching an array of video monitors; the screens displaying the faces of the returning dead, lying buried in the earth.

Dellamorte couldn't imagine anything more boring. The dead were tedious enough when they were up and moving about. The way he saw it, he was about to do the man a huge favour.

The click of his revolver quickly alerted the technician to Dellamorte's presence. When he saw the gun trained upon him, he began to gibber. *Please! This is very important work we're doing here!*

I don't care, said Dellamorte, terminating the exchange with a single gunshot.

The man had been whiling away the wee hours with a good bottle of wine, so Dellamorte took the remainder for himself, before grabbing a couple of cans of petrol he found onsite and methodically dousing the area with their contents.

As he retreated to a safe distance to watch the building burn, he took a swig of wine and mused aloud. *What now, my love? More smoke signals?*

But as the flames continued to spread across the area, the billowing clouds of gasoline smoke stubbornly refused to form into a recognisable shape, try as Dellamorte might to discern any meaningful pattern. Blinking back tears caused by the drifting fumes, he wondered if he was going mad.

Perhaps that had even been Death's intention all along.

He raised the bottle to his lips once more, only for it to shatter in his hand, drenching him in red wine. As he gazed down at his sopping, ruined shirt, he thought he heard a coldly insinuating chuckle.

Wine? Was *that* the clue? Dellamorte had no patience for these tediously cryptic puzzles. He began to wonder whether he should have agreed to a game of chess after all.

Two weeks later, Dellamorte arrived in southern France. He had heard stories of an abandoned vineyard in the town of Roubelais, rumoured to be infested with the undead. This time the plague had allegedly been caused by experimental pesticides infecting the local grape crop. Dellamorte could only marvel at the ever-more ridiculous rationales people could invent to explain away the returning dead. He took a certain measure of pride in the fact that he was a simple man, not much given to overthinking matters. It was not, he decided, for him to reason why.

After he had cleansed the vineyard, he wearily made his way into Roubelais, now largely reduced to a ghost town. The only sign of life he could see was an old blind beggar standing alone on a street corner, forlornly rattling a tin can.

Dellamorte had a few francs left in his pocket, so he wandered over and deposited them in the man's cup. The beggar gifted him a grateful smile ripe with decay and nodded his head in silent thanks. Dellamorte was about to move off in search of a bed for the night when he realised the man was busily scratching something in the earth with his walking stick. He watched as a crude symbol gradually took shape, eventually recognising it as an Egyptian ankh.

Oh, for Christ's sake, Dellamorte groaned. When would this torture ever end?

The beggar slowly shuffled away, leaving Dellamorte to contemplate this latest enigma.

The clue eventually took him to a small town on the Spanish coastline, where he engaged in the first of a number of skirmishes with a Satanic sect of undead Templars, the so-called Blind Dead. Here, at last, was an opponent that finally tested his mettle. The Templars' fighting prowess and their unearthly ability to locate their prey by sound made them deadly adversaries. And although he managed to triumph in their first encounter, Dellamorte quickly learned of the existence of other Templar burial sites throughout Spain.

Relishing the challenge ahead, his ongoing quest led him to the ruins of the medieval town of Berzano, a locus for the undead cult. Here, he was lucky to escape with his life, the Blind Dead overwhelming him with sheer force of numbers and pursuing him through the countryside on their skeletal steeds.

It appeared Death had temporarily gained the upper hand.

Licking his wounds, Dellamorte retreated to

plan his next move. He decided to head for civilisation, to the city of Lisbon, for once eager to surround himself with the teeming vibrancy of urban life. It suddenly felt as though there was such a thing as too much death, even for him.

He took a room at one of the best hotels in town, and decided to spend an evening refreshing himself in the bar. The appearance of this ragged, sallow wraith attracted more than a little attention amongst the bar's patrons, and Dellamorte quickly sequestered himself in its darkest corner, so as to be left to drown his sorrows in peace.

But, as he was soon to discover, there were other travellers frequenting the bar that night who also favoured the shadows.

Upon finishing his first glass of wine, Dellamorte glanced up to find an attractive blonde woman standing over his table, studying him. Carrying an ageless air of aristocratic languor, she wore a figure-hugging silver lamé dress, which glittered in the dim candlelight like a thousand eyes. Her almost hypnotic allure was evident to all who laid eyes on her; still, normally Dellamorte might not have given her a second glance. These days, he only had eyes for Death.

However, there was something about her, some intangible quality...

Good evening, the woman said. *I do hope I'm not disturbing you.*

Her voice was low and indolent. Dellamorte thought he detected the trace of an accent, something eastern European and to his ears, vaguely exotic.

I'm not usually much of a one for company, he replied. *But for you, madame, I shall gladly make an exception.*

He got to his feet, pulled out the chair opposite him, and invited her to sit. Retaking his own seat, he studied her face, fascinated despite himself.

She stared back at him, unblinking. *You're a traveller,* she said.

I suppose you could say that.

Whereabouts are you travelling to?

I don't know yet. I'm searching for someone.

Who?

Oh, it's a long story. How could be possibly explain his quest to her?

The woman motioned for the waiter to bring them more wine. *But I like long stories. When you've lived a life as protracted as mine, you're always keen to find ways to pass the time.*

Fuck it, he decided. *I'm searching for Death*, Dellamorte admitted. *She's been leading me a merry dance for a while now, but I think I'm getting close.*

He expected the woman to laugh in his face, to call him mad and flee to the other end of the bar, but instead, she continued to gaze at him with the same unwavering, serpentine look, which Dellamorte was, by now, beginning to find somewhat perturbing.

Well, it appears we have a mutual acquaintance, she said finally, her eyes glinting with sly amusement.

You know her? Dellamorte said, incredulous.

Oh, we've been friends for a great many years now. I'm on my way to meet her, in fact.

He could not believe his good fortune, not after the interminable trials of the last few months. Perhaps his long quest was finally at an end. *Could you...could you take me with you?*

She considered. *I don't see why not. You seem like a charming enough young man.*

Success! The waiter appeared with a fresh bottle of wine for them, which Dellamorte accepted eagerly. Hurriedly pouring a measure into their two glasses, he raised his in a toast. *To newfound travelling companions,* he said.

The woman smiled. *I think perhaps if we're going to be companions, we should first be properly introduced,* she said.

Dellamorte held up his hands apologetically. *You're quite right. I'm sorry, I'm getting completely ahead of myself. I'm Francesco Dellamorte, and I'm very pleased to meet you...?*

My name is Elizabeta, she replied.

Thus introduced, they made a toast to their nascent friendship, before Dellamorte's lustful impatience got the better of him.

So, Elizabeta, when do you think we can leave? he asked his new companion.

Something blossomed in her gaze, something warm and red, like an artery being opened in a hot bath. Dellamorte found himself plunging helplessly down into those bottomless crimson waters, and the deeper he descended, the less he cared – about life, death or anything. He wanted only to swim there forever.

Oh, but I think I'll have some fun with you first, Elizabeth Báthory said.

Countess Elizabeth Báthory

Delphine Seyrig in *Les lèvres rouge*
(Daughters of Darkness), 1971
written by J.J. Amiel, Pierre Drouot and Harry Kümel
directed by Harry Kümel

After she had taken a lover to bed for the first time, Elizabeth Báthory would always tell them the same story. As her *inamorato* lay sprawled naked across the bedclothes like a child's soft toy, enraptured and bleeding, she would cradle their head in her lap and recount to them the sad tale of her birth. Not her entrance into the world as a squalling, still-innocent child, mind – for even the Bloody Countess was innocent once – but her *true* day of creation, the moment where she was set free to embrace her terrible destiny.

As Michaelangelo once said, every block of stone has a statue concealed inside, and it is simply the sculptor's task to discover it. Before she encountered the foul creature that created her, Elizabeth Báthory was as that block of stone; shapeless and unformed. However, as the great artist suggested, perhaps she was always fated to become the monster that was unleashed that day, and it took only the intervention of Count Orlok to release the malign potential that had lain dormant inside her ever since she drew her first breath.

Francesco Dellamorte was no different from any of her other suitors. He had been seduced, bled, and was now sprawled helplessly across the tousled covers of the Countess's hotel bed. Suspended in a hypnotic fugue, he was cognisant of very little, save for the cool breeze wafting in through the open doors to the balcony, the soothing amniotic sound of the ocean waters in the harbour below, and Elizabeth's soft purr, as she whispered long-forgotten secrets into his ear.

It was the early days of the Thirteen Years' War, she began. *My husband Ferenc was away fighting the Ottomans, and in his absence, it fell to me to manage his business affairs, which included control of his many estates. Those were perilous times, my love. His lands were located along the trade route to Vienna, and several villages had already been attacked and looted by the Turks. Our forces were horribly depleted by the war, and I was at a loss as to how I would protect our land and people.*

Then I received a letter from another Hungarian nobleman, Count Orlok. He loathed the Ottomans with a bilious passion that might even have exceeded our own, and was offering the use of his armies to help defend our homelands. Perhaps I would like to travel to his castle in the Carpathians to discuss the matter in more depth?

I imagine that vile demon is all but unknown to your Western history books, but in my day simply to whisper his name was considered akin to spreading a plague. They called him the Bird of Death, and it was said that he had been created by Belial, one of the most terrible Kings of Hell.

Of course, I was a noblewoman and considered myself far above such ignorant superstitions. Still, I knew full well it did not necessarily require Hell's intervention to create vicious, evil men; enough of them had sat at our own banquet table for me to recognise that humanity possessed its own infinitely diabolic potential. I understood that Orlok was dangerous and not to be trusted, and yet my loyalty to my husband and my people drove me to seek out his aid regardless. After all, I told myself, Count Orlok would not dare risk incurring the wrath of the commander-in-chief of the entire Hungarian Army! I would travel with a number of bodyguards and retainers, and was quite certain I would be safe.

What a fool I was!

After a long, arduous journey through the mountains, we arrived at the Count's castle just as the sun was setting. In the red light of dusk, the valley below the fortress appeared to be awash with blood; little did I suspect it was a dire premonition of what was to come.

Orlok himself greeted us at the castle gates. I had of course heard the legends of his hideous appearance, but nothing could have prepared me for the verminous apparition that awaited me. When I first laid eyes on him, I thought for one awful moment that he was nothing but a skeleton made somehow animate; all flesh appeared to have been stripped from the leering death's head that passed for his face. As I drew closer I realised I was mistaken; some meat did still cling to his bones, but it was wasted and grey in pallor, as though he were a corpse long overdue for burial. I can only describe his features as a skull beneath a skull. He possessed two long rat-like teeth that protruded horribly over his bottom lip, and pale, long-fingered hands that put me in mind of some repulsive albino spider. Indeed, he moved like some great predatory insect; frozen with the stillness of the grave one instant, but capable of incredible speed the next.

He welcomed us inside and showed us to a dining table laden with a great feast. The food and wine were excellent, but despite our long journey, we could muster little appetite. Even the hardiest of my protectors had been sorely shaken by the sight of Orlok, and the tangible pall of corruption that hung over the castle had the effect of rendering even the most delicious meal all but inedible.

Orlok watched us as we picked listlessly at our food, eating nothing himself. Once we had finished, he showed us to our rooms, telling me that I should rest well for the night, and that we would attend to our business on the morrow, once I was fully refreshed.

I remember thinking that the apparent lack of servants in the castle was decidedly curious, but put it down to the cloud of superstition that surrounded the Count; in truth, now that I had breathed the same fetid air as Orlok, those wild stories seemed much less fanciful.

Despite being exhausted by my travels, I slept fitfully, plagued by uneasy dreams. I awoke in the dead of night, the oppressive silence of the castle crushing me like a vice. I lay there in the darkness and prayed for a sound to reach my ears. Any sound would suffice, even the faintest scratching of rats' claws; anything to reassure me I was still drawing breath and not trapped in some dreadful black limbo of endless quietude.

But the ghastly noise that came next made a mockery of such pitiful fears; better some mute purgatory than the horror of hearing the bravest of my men shrieking like a frightened child. His torment seemed almost without end; I wished only that the agonising pitch of his cries might shatter my eardrums, so that I would have to suffer them no longer. I wanted to flee, but heavy chains could not have bound me to my bed any tighter than the dread that appalling sound induced. I could only lie there helplessly and wait, knowing that whatever evil had prompted that scream would soon come for me.

Then, finally, silence settled once more upon the castle like a dark snowfall. When my chamber door did open moments later, it was quietly, almost respectfully, as though my visitor did not wish to alarm me by the untoward manner of his entrance. My eyes moved to the doorway, and what I beheld there left me longing that I had been struck deaf and blind both.

Orlok stood poised over my bed, his long fingers clawing the air like tree branches in the dead of winter. In the dim moonlight, his face and hands appeared slathered with ink; of course, blood appears quite black beneath the radiance of the moon. Upon meeting my gaze, he grinned horribly, his mouth widening until it split his face like a chasm. It contorted and stretched until it swallowed me, the room, everything.

For the whole of that night, and the two following it, Orlok violated my body and soul. After four long centuries, I can still recall vividly every last obscenity he visited upon me. He left me too weak to resist or escape, and I had no doubt my retinue were already dead by his hand. In whatever brief moments of respite he allowed me, he would lay curled against my naked body like a parasite, his skin like cold, pitted clay, and whisper abject secrets into my ear; an education in damnation.

I thought I would die in that accursed place, but at the end of our third night together, he rose from the bed and told me I was free to go. Of course, I had not the strength to even crawl to the bedroom door, and as he took his leave, I fell into a swoon, a long, feverish dream of dead things. I imagined I was surrounded by all those I had lost; my beloved mother and father, the faithful servants I had brought with me to the castle. But although I found myself amongst the dead, I was not of them, and as I beseeched them for help, one by one, they silently turned their backs on me.

When I awoke from the nightmare, my first thought was that I was still trapped in that same damned bed, in that same damned room, in that same damned castle. But then I felt the wind on my bare skin and the prickle of grass against my cheek, and I knew something had changed.

I opened my eyes and somehow found myself on the hillside in front of my own home, Čachtice Castle, naked and alone.

A guard quickly spotted me, and I was rushed inside by servants and placed in my bed. I was still on the brink of death, wracked by delirium, and it was thought that I might not survive.

But survive I did – in a manner of speaking. After many days of rest, I was still terribly weak, my flesh bloodless and atrophied; but my mind had at last cleared and I now knew what I must do.

I summoned a maidservant and instructed her to draw me a bath, so that I might be cleansed of the sweat and stink of my fever. After she had helped me into the tub and commenced bathing me, I took a hairpin and stabbed her in the throat.

What issued forth was purer and more delicious than the clearest spring from the highest mountain peak. Once I had drunk my fill, I allowed her remaining life to drain into my bathwater.

And within minutes, I was born anew; my youth, beauty and vitality were restored, even enhanced.

That is a true story, my love, or as true as I can make it after so many long centuries have passed. I swore vengeance on Orlok if our paths ever crossed again, but alas, his foulness was expunged from the world before my chance arrived. But from that day on, I allowed no man to insult or harm me ever again. I saw to it that even the smallest of slights were met with the most terrible of reprisals.

And as for the rest, it is, as they say, history...

Her tale complete, the Countess rose from the bed and began to gather her clothes, chiding her lover as she dressed. *Look at the time! I've prattled on for far too long. It's entirely your fault for being such a good listener, Francesco.*

Still lying motionless on the mattress, Dellamorte let out a sound that was somewhere between a sigh of pleasure and a moan of utter despair.

Hush now, Elizabeth told him. *You really must pull yourself together, my dear. I'm due in Ostend in three days and I need you to drive the car. And once we arrive, you will finally meet the woman you've been seeking. Won't that be exciting?*

So for the next three nights, they made their

way up through Europe, stopping to rest by day. The Countess continued to bleed Dellamorte as they travelled, but was careful not to allow her hunger to get the better of her, lest she cause irreparable harm to her mistress's intended.

When they finally arrived at their destination, the Grand Hôtel des Thermes, situated on the Ostend beachfront, Elizabeth gazed up at its stately *belle époque* facade with evident delight.

Isn't it divine, Francesco? It was my idea to hold our meeting here. I try to return every fifty years or so. This lovely old hotel seems to exist apart from the world somehow, forever fixed and unchanging. I find that so reassuring in today's society, so obsessed with damnable modernity and change for the sake of change.

Dellamorte mumbled in rote agreement and began the long process of transporting Elizabeth's numerous items of baggage inside. The Countess herself swept into the reception area like a glittering tide, murmuring with delight when she saw the wizened-looking hotel clerk standing expectantly behind the front desk. *My dear man! Are you still here after all these years?*

The clerk's aged features lit up at the sight of the Countess. *Madame Báthory, what a great pleasure it is to see you again. I had heard there had been a terrible accident the last time you were with us...*

The Countess nonchalantly waved him away. *Oh, that. Just a momentary inconvenience. When you've lived as long as I have, it's good to change bodies every century or so anyway...*

The clerk looked wistful. *Alas, madame, I am stuck with the one I have, failing and decrepit though it is.*

Dellamorte appeared at Elizabeth's side, depositing several suitcases in front of the desk. The clerk looked at him with evident dismay, then murmured an aside to the Countess. *Ah, madame, there is a small problem. When they booked out the hotel for the weekend, the three mesdames stipulated that no male guests were permitted...*

Elizabeth smiled. *Do not worry, my dear. This one is a gift for La Mere de les Ténèbres, oui? I shall escort him to her room now.*

The clerk nodded, reassured. *Very good, madame. As for your own room, I have placed you next to Madame Vajda? I believe you two have much in common.*

He held out a room key, which Elizabeth accepted with a wordless nod. She was not fond of Asa Vajda. Despite the fact that they were about the same age, on their occasional encounters the other woman tended to treat the Countess like a younger sibling, there only to be humoured and tolerated. Elizabeth did not respond at all well to being patronised by a commoner witch.

She joined arms with her escort and led him up the grand staircase towards the hotel suites. When they reached the correct floor, Elizabeth noticed a distinct smell of almonds in the air, and a sudden drop in temperature. She escorted Dellamorte to the door at the end of the hallway, then knocked gently to announce their arrival.

Mother? It is I, Elizabeta. I come bearing gifts...

The door opened without a sound, revealing an interior so devoid of light it might have been a yawning abyss, plunging away into nothingness.

Elizabeth gave Dellamorte a gentle nudge, encouraging him forwards. *Go on, my dear. She is waiting for you.*

A dawning awareness sparked in Dellamorte's eyes, and he began to stumble backwards, suddenly afraid. *No...*

A sepulchral voice then announced itself from inside the room, ringing out like a funeral bell. *Dellamorte! Come to me! It is time to claim your prize!*

Dellamorte tried to resist, but as much as his conscious mind struggled against Mater Tenebrarum's command, his helpless body found itself compelled by it. Hands vainly flailing about, eyes bulging in horror, his legs carried him across the threshold, where he was soon consumed by the waiting void.

As the Countess watched him vanish from sight, the hotel room door silently closed once more. Her task accomplished, she turned and briskly made her way back down the corridor, only missing a fraction of a step when she heard Dellamorte's despairing scream quickly rise and fall behind her, like a lone firework in the night sky.

When she arrived at her own room, she was about to turn her key in the lock when she heard someone emerging from the adjacent doorway. Glancing around, she was shocked to see an imposing-looking man exiting Asa Vajda's hotel room. Dressed in an expensive Italian suit and carrying an ebony cane in one hand, he was heavily-bearded, with long black hair worn in a ponytail. When his eyes met Elizabeth's, he gave a smile that might have been a wolfish snarl, and bowed his head in greeting. *Madame*, he said reverently.

The Countess was too stunned to reply, and could only watch as he strolled casually past her and towards the staircase. Hurrying inside her room, she picked up the phone and dialled reception, the clerk answering in an instant. *Madame Báthory?*

Listen to me. There is another man in the hotel, she snapped. *I just saw him coming out of Madame Vajda's room.*

I shall look into the matter immediately, madame, the clerk replied.

Satisfied for the moment, she hung up. She was tempted to investigate the situation herself, but the sun was beginning to rise outside the hotel windows, which would limit both her and Asa Vajda's movements for the duration of the daylight hours. Disconcerted by her encounter with the strange man, she resigned herself to ignorance for the time being, drew the heavy curtains against the dawn and retired to bed.

~

When the Countess returned downstairs later that evening, she went immediately to the front desk to enquire if there was any further information pertaining to Asa Vajda's visitor.

The old clerk was apologetic. *I did not learn much, madame. He told me he was a very old friend of Madame Vajda's, and that their paths had unexpectedly crossed in Ostend. When I informed him the entire hotel was booked for a private function and that no male guests were allowed, he apologised and gave me a rather large tip for the inconvenience.*

And his name?

I believe it was Monsieur Cyphre, madame.

On the face of it, the name meant absolutely nothing to the Countess, and yet something still troubled her. Regardless, she thanked the clerk and gave him a large tip to add to the one he had already received, which he accepted gratefully. *The others are already gathering in the ballroom,* he informed her.

Elizabeth proceeded to the meeting room to find it thronged with women of all ages and nationalities; women whose very names inspired awe and dread in countries across the world. Many were unknown to her, but amongst those she recognised were Marguerite Chopin, the lady Leonor, Irena Dubrovna, Elizabeth's old rival the Countess Marya Zaleska, the Black Bride Julie Kohler, Santanico Pandemonium, who appeared to be competing with Irina von Karlstein for the title of least-dressed, Daniella Neseri, the mermaids named Mora and Golden, and the Finnish were-reindeer Pirita.

The Countess marvelled at such an assemblage of arcane feminine power in one single room. Surely there could be no limit as to what they might achieve together!

Emerging from the crowd at the far end of the ballroom, Elizabeth took up a position in front of the empty stage, upon which were placed three chairs, placed in readiness for the arrival of the Three Mothers. As the Countess patiently awaited their entrance, she suddenly became aware of a watchful presence at her side, and turned to see Asa Vajda herself.

The woman smiled at Elizabeth, which had the effect of reminding her of a grinning, hollow-eyed skull. *Soră*, Asa said, with none of the sisterly affection the word implied.

Hello Asa, the Countess replied.

You have been interfering in my affairs, I think.

Elizabeth's face darkened. *You know no men are allowed here.*

Asa rolled her huge eyes. *You should mind your business, Countess. He was of no importance to you. Just an old lover.*

If the Mothers should find out...

But they won't. Will they? She stared defiantly back at the Countess, the implied threat unmistakeable.

In response, Elizabeth took an aggressive step towards her, only for Asa to hiss warningly. *Tsk. Not here, Countess. Not now. We are all sisters today, are we not?*

The two women glared at each other, neither willing to back down, until their stand-off was interrupted by the lowering of the ballroom lights. Asa Vajda momentarily forgotten, the Countess turned to see two figures walk onstage: the cloaked silhouette of Mater Tenebrarum, forever wreathed in shadow; and the eternally-beautiful Mater Lachrymarum, resplendent in an ice-blue gown. Beside them, a spectral impression of a third woman began to coalesce in the air; Mater Suspiriorum, still without physical form after the destruction of her body decades before, but as equally wicked and all-powerful as her two sisters nonetheless.

Impassioned applause broke out amongst the crowd. As she joined the approbation, the Countess silently registered the gleaming skull the Mother of Darkness cradled in her lap like a new toy.

Alas, poor Dellamorte...

Mater Lachrymarum motioned for quiet. *Daughters,* she began. *We are gathered here on neutral ground today, to address the growing threat that endangers us all. Let no past feuds or rivalries interfere with our business here. That is in the past. We must be united as one, against He who would seek to divide and rule us all.*

As you are all aware, a calamitous war has been looming for some years. Having failed in his bid to conquer the world of man through his puppet king the Antichrist, Lucifer seeks to deny us assuming that throne for ourselves. For thousands of years, he has subjugated us women; enslaved us, violated and abused us. And now, he schemes to rob us of the emancipation we have struggled so long to make a reality.

There were murmurs of disquiet amongst the audience. The Mother of Tears continued:

Who here has not been defiled by this creature? Have any of you escaped His obscene attentions? Identify yourself, if you have so been blessed.

No one stepped forward.

When the world was young, He visited my sisters and I in turn. And one by one, he violated us all. Demeaned and humiliated us in the foulest of ways, simply because He demanded it as His due. We were not powerful enough to defy Him then, but much has changed in the years since. Now, together, we can resist Lucifer! We can triumph!

A mass of cheers broke out in the room, gradually subsiding as Mater Lachrymarum's expression became grave.

I cannot lie to you. The battle that lies ahead will be savage and bloody. He will not surrender meekly, not to mere women. Already He has begun to strike at us, murdering our valued disciples via deception and trickery. Still, our defensive wards have held fast against Him, and He remains ignorant as to the location of our remaining sanctum. For as long as its whereabouts are hidden from Him, we can offer sanctuary to any of you who feel under threat from His forces. Have no fear, the Three Mothers will protect all of their faithful children.

A frightened voice from the audience: *Yes, I*

have felt His foul breath on my neck! I know He is watching me! Where is this sanctuary, Mother?

This prompted a wave of alarmed whispers, until Mater Lachrymarum gestured for calm. *Listen to me, daughter. Come to Rome, to the Hotel Levana. There is room for you all in our home. You will be safe from Lucifer. Join us there, so that we may plan our uprising together!*

There was further applause, but plagued by an insistent feeling of disquiet, Elizabeth did not join in. Glancing around, she noticed that Asa Vajda had vanished.

Then it struck her. The tawdry joke that had eluded her understanding until now.

Monsieur Cyphre. *Lucifer.*

Asa Vajda was in league with the Devil.

No! The Countess cried out in despair, and turned to bolt from the room, shoving her bewildered sisters aside as she set out in pursuit of the treacherous witch who sought to betray them. Noticing the timid figure of Irena Dubrovna lurking by the ballroom entrance, Elizabeth grabbed her arm. *Come on, I need your help!*

Dragging the startled girl behind her, the Countess emerged into the hotel lobby, where the clerk lay stunned on the floor, bleeding from his temple. Weakly, he pointed towards the exit, gesturing at the beachfront beyond.

The two women burst from the hotel in time to see Asa fleeing down the steps towards the sea. A dark figure awaited her there, drawing circles in the sand with his cane.

We'll never catch her in time, breathed Elizabeth. *Or at least, I won't.*

She turned to Irena, whose eyes widened in dismay. *I c-can't just change,* she stammered. *That isn't how it works...*

Oh, I know, my dear...

The Countess pulled Irena close and kissed her. Despite her well-known proclivities, she actually found the prospect of kissing the Serbian peasant girl rather revolting; Irena was attractive enough in a vulgar sort of way, but to Báthory's heightened senses, she smelled like exactly what she was – a wild beast.

Still, this was no time to be picky.

As the Countess's sensuous hands began to caress her body, Irena moaned and shuddered, attempting to pull away. But only when she was sure the inevitable transformation was underway did Elizabeth finally consent to release the girl from their embrace.

What have you done? Irena whimpered, her dress beginning to tear, her flesh contorting and thickening with fur.

Merely what was required. Now it's your turn, the Countess replied, pointing down towards Asa.

Elizabeth watched with fascination as Irena completed her metamorphosis into a large black panther. Its taut sinews thrumming with barely-suppressed fury, the big cat let out a roar and bounded down the steps in pursuit of its prey.

Asa looked back over her shoulder and cried out in fear, quickening her pace as she attempted to cross the remaining distance towards her master in time. But the heavy pull of the sand on her feet slowed her, and the pursuing panther easily closed the gap separating them. It pounced, its claws ripping into Asa's back and yanking her down onto the beach.

Good girl, whispered Elizabeth, hurrying down the steps after them. She looked on in satisfaction as the panther frenziedly proceeded to reduce Asa to meat and bone. The Countess couldn't imagine that four-hundred-year-old flesh tasted particularly appetising, but that didn't seem to deter Irena from her feast.

Her eyes moved to the Devil, who seemed content to keep a safe distance and calmly watch His acolyte die; at least, until the moment Elizabeth finally reached the bottom of the steps, when He suddenly broke into stride, marched across the sand, lifted His cane, and used it to fatally spear the attacking beast through the heart.

Elizabeth and the panther howled in unison. By the time the Countess arrived at her side, Irena was already transforming back to her human form, the cane buried deep in her chest, pinning her like a butterfly. Choking on her own blood, she looked imploringly up at Elizabeth, who gently took the stricken girl in her arms and cradled her as she died.

After Irena had breathed her last, the Countess looked up to see the Devil squatting on His haunches next to Asa, listening intently to his mortally-injured disciple's dying words. He offered Asa no other solace as she, too, fled from this world into the next.

The Countess picked herself up and warily approached the Devil, who rose to meet her.

Countess Báthory. He looked genuinely pleased to see her. *It's been far too long.*

Elizabeth did not reciprocate. *Get out of here,* she told Him. *You're not welcome in this place.*

The Devil shrugged. *No matter. Asa survived long enough to give me her message.* He smirked. *Ah well, at least I got to enjoy her pale little body one last time.*

You pig! The Countess lashed out and slapped Him, her sharp nails drawing blood from his cheek.

The Devil cackled in glee. Grotesquely, His tongue slithered from His mouth and began to slide across His cheek. Impossibly long, twisting like a pink worm emerging from the earth, it licked greedily at the bleeding wound.

Elizabeth looked away, repulsed.

I'll see you in Rome, the Devil jeered.

The next moment, He was gone.

Mater Suspiriorum
Lela Svasta in *Suspiria*, 1977
written by Dario Argento & Daria Nicolodi
directed by Dario Argento

Mater Tenebrarum
Veronica Lazar in *Inferno*, 1980
written & directed by Dario Argento

Mater Lachrymarum
Ania Pieroni in *Inferno*, 1980
written & directed by Dario Argento

The sinister history of the Three Mothers has already been exhaustively chronicled by the alchemist Varelli, and need be of little concern to us here. For anyone interested in learning more of their many secrets, I would recommend you try and procure a copy of his fascinating book on the subject. (Beware, however; it has long been rumoured that the work is cursed, and that great harm may come to anyone who reads it.)

No, for the present, we need only occupy ourselves with where their story is now.

That, and the ending that is still yet to be written.

Mater Lachrymarum gazed down from the penthouse balcony at the undead battalion massed below like a plague of locusts, poised to devour and destroy anything in their path. The dawn sky was red with impending bloodshed, and somewhere in the distance, a church bell tolled.

The Mother of Tears turned to her sisters and spoke. *The time is at hand. Do we fight and perish, or bow to Him as he demands?*

Mater Tenebrarum spat a reply. *I will never bow to Him again. Licking His filthy asshole once was enough.*

Each of the sisters fought back revulsion as they recalled the humiliation of the *Osculum infame*, the Devil's preferred ritual greeting. That vile memory alone was enough to bolster their resolve. They had toiled for centuries to achieve the power they currently enjoyed; to surrender it all to the loathsome abuser who had defiled them and so many of their daughters was unthinkable.

And you, sister? Mater Lachrymarum asked her oldest sibling.

Mater Suspiriorum's disembodied voice swept through the room like a graveyard wind. *Fight,* she said.

Then it is settled, her sister said.

War had begun.

In response to the Three Mother's defiance, the Devil had called his most pitiless warriors to arms: the regiment of undead Templars known as the Blind Dead. The army had ridden across Europe, massacring everything that lay before them, until finally the dead entered Rome and laid siege to the Hotel Levana, the Three Mothers' sole remaining lair.

Anticipating the attack, the sisters had withdrawn the entirety of their own forces to the building; the diaspora of faithful daughters who served them in countless countries across the globe, and the scores of deadly black-gloved assassins the Mothers used to carry out their murderous bidding.

But would it be enough? The Three Mothers possessed immense power, but their acolytes were sorely outnumbered. Moreover, their soulless opponents were incapable of feeling fear or dismay; the morale of the undead was implacable, monolithic in its utter steadfastness.

Nevertheless, all were in agreement that it was far better to risk death than suffer the abject submission Lucifer would demand if they capitulated to Him. For a being whose own diabolical will had been forged in the white-hot flames of defiance, He was singularly intolerant of dissent amongst His own ranks. The Three Mothers knew any punishment they underwent at His hands would be legendary in its ruthlessness, boundless in its duration.

Mater Lachrymarum returned to the edge of the balcony, gazing out beyond the gathered Templar ranks. She could see a distant figure reclining on a cafe terrace on the other side of the square, a cocktail clasped in his hand. As she watched, the Devil raised his glass in mocking salute.

The other two sisters moved to Mater Lachrymarum's side. Together as one, they joined hands – those of them that still possessed hands – and shrieked an unearthly howl of affront to the skies, a screaming call to battle so devastating in its elemental power that it shattered eardrums across the city – not to mention the Devil's cocktail glass, in the precise moment he was raising the frosted rim to his lips.

He accepted this slight with equanimity. He had charged his Cenobites with devising several exquisitely vicious methods of retribution to welcome the Three Mothers upon their imminent arrival in Hell, and was already relishing the suffering that was to come. He therefore decided He could afford to overlook this final paltry insult. With a shrug, the Devil tossed away the broken shards of the glass and took up a position from which to observe the coming massacre.

The fighting raged for several days, and Rome's gutters were soon overflowing with women's blood and the putrefied flesh of the Templars. Even the heavens themselves seemed to dread the outcome of the battle; after the sun set upon the first day of the conflict, it would not rise again until all hostility had ended; a portentously apocalyptic phenomenon that could surely only have been prompted by Mater

Tenebrarum's hand. Across the city, slews of civilians threw themselves from tall buildings or opened up their veins in warm bathtubs; hundreds more engaged in insane bacchanals, drinking, fucking and fighting in the streets. On the third day of combat, when Mater Lachrymarum looked out upon the scores of her fallen daughters littering the city streets and began to weep, the entire surviving population of Rome were instantly seized by uncontrollable fits of crying.

Over the course of the fierce struggle, there were many instances of heroic triumph, punctuated by occasions of the bleakest despair. Amongst the former, we might include the discovery that the Templars' enhanced hearing made them acutely susceptible to the siren song of the mermaids; all Mora and Golden had to do was lie in wait in the large ornamental water fountain in the middle of the square and lure the undead within easy reach, whereupon they easily tore them to shreds. Or the daring raid devised by the Black Bride, when she secretly led a team of assassins through the city sewers to emerge in position behind the ranks of the unsuspecting Templars, several of whom quickly succumbed to the deadly ambush from below.

Of the latter, no one who witnessed the event will forget the bloodthirsty hunt that erupted on the second day, when the Devil led a troop of mounted Templars in unrelenting pursuit of Pirita around the nearby streets; after they finally drove the were-reindeer to exhaustion and collapse, the horsebacked troops proceeded to sadistically trample her to death. Or the moment when the undead soldiers captured the lynx-eyed temptress who had betrayed Dean Corso in London; in retaliation for her treachery, the Devil ordered her strung up from a lamppost and allowed the ravenous Templars to batten on her.

There were all these deaths and countless more, far too many to record here. But then, miraculously, the war was over.

Despite their deficit in numbers, the Three Mothers' army had fought with a desperate, unmatched fury, and had succeeded in battling the Devil's legion to a complete standstill. When the fighting finally ceased, hardly a single Templar had survived. This was not to say the Mothers hadn't suffered their own grievous losses; of the hundreds of followers that had commenced the conflict, only a dozen or so were left standing by its end. Worse yet, the Three Mothers knew their own reserves were completely exhausted, whereas their malefic tormentor could surely summon up further multitudes of hellspawn with but a casual wave of his hand.

Regardless, their resistance had been emphatic, and a victory of sorts had been achieved. If they were to die now, it would be in full possession of the dignity that the Devil had always denied them.

The Mothers instructed their few remaining acolytes to stand down, and strode out on the battlefield to parley with their opponent. The Devil sat atop a piled heap of Templar corpses, calmly sucking a lollipop. As the sisters approached Him, he gave a sardonic genuflection and applauded.

Bravo! he said. *You have fought bravely, sisters.*

And shall continue to do so, Mater Lachrymarum replied.

The Devil pulled an exasperated face. *God, aren't you bored with all this? I, for one, have certainly got much better things to do.*

It appeared that patience was not one of the Devil's (scant) virtues.

What are you suggesting? said Mater Tenebrarum. *A settlement?*

Perhaps, perhaps, the Devil mused. *There must be a mutually acceptable outcome. Things have got rather hysterical, wouldn't you say?*

Mater Lachrymarum's cold eyes flared with sudden fire. *We will settle for nothing less than the world being surrendered to our complete control. Furthermore, you will undertake not to set foot on Earth for as long as we deem it appropriate.*

And what makes you think you're in a position to demand such a thing, my dear? the Devil retorted.

With every day this war continues, the weaker you appear, she told him. *Good luck with trying to tempt anyone over to your side after this. Don't you see? Even if you were to win, you've already lost. The almighty Prince of Darkness, held at bay by a mob of hysterical women!*

The Devil growled and spat in contempt, his saliva hitting the blood-soaked pavement with a sizzle. *If I agree, nothing more will be spoken of this. I will not have my esteemed reputation besmirched by a coven of turncoat whores. You and your sisters will use your influence to cloud the minds of the entire world. It will be as though none of this ever happened.*

Agreed, the Mothers said in unison.

And like that, it was decided.

The Devil climbed wearily to his feet and looked around with a sigh. *You know, I'll miss the old place. Still, perhaps when you ladies have all calmed down a bit...?*

The Three Mothers held their tongues.

Their opponent shrugged. Turning to leave, he paused halfway and glanced back at the Mother of Tears. *You were always the loveliest of them, my dear*, he told her wistfully. *Seeing as I've been such a gentleman about everything, I don't suppose there's any chance of a final merry-go-round before I'm on my way? We could head up to your honeymoon suite and take a long hot soak in the tub together...?* He smiled seductively, and held out a hand to her.

You know precisely where you can go, she replied.

In response, the Devil giggled like a child, and immediately transformed Himself into the ethereal figure of a young girl, dressed all in white. As the Mothers watched, the girl picked up the severed head of a Templar, and, tossing it in the air like a ball, skipped happily away down the street, frolicking off into exile.

He was entirely content to let the Three Mothers think they had won, for now. For what they did not know was that His son Damien, the Antichrist, was newly resurgent again after his crushing defeat of several decades before.

The Devil still had a foothold on Earth after all.

And the bitter war between men and women would go on, and on, and on.

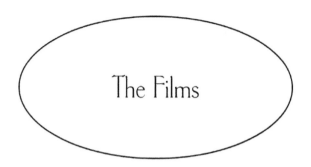

The Films

Angel Heart (1987)
Betty Blue (1986)
     aka 37°2 le matin
The Black Cat (1934)
The Bride Wore Black (1968)
     aka La mariée était en noir
Burial Ground (1981)
     aka Le notti del terrore
Cat People (1942)
Cemetery Man (1994)
     aka Dellamorte Dellamore
Color Me Blood Red (1965)
Daughters of Darkness (1971)
     aka Les lèvres rouges
Dracula's Daughter (1936)
Female Vampire (1973)
From Dusk Till Dawn (1996)
The Grapes of Death (1978)
     aka Les raisins de la mort

Hellraiser (1987)

The House of Exorcism (1975)
aka La casa dell'esorcismo

The House with Laughing Windows (1976)
aka La casa dalle finestre che ridono

Inferno (1980)

Inside (2007)
aka À l'interieur

Kill, Baby... Kill! (1966)
aka Operazione paura

The Last Temptation of Christ (1988)

Lisa and the Devil (1974)
aka Lisa e il diavolo

Leonor (1975)

The Lure (2015)
aka Córki dancingu

The Mask of Satan (1960)
aka La maschera del demonio

Night Tide (1961)

Night of the Seagulls (1975)
aka La noche de las gaviotas

The Ninth Gate (1999)

Nosferatu: A Symphony of Horror (1922)
aka Nosferatu, eine symphonie des grauens

The Omen (1976)

Omen III: The Final Conflict (1981)

The Perfume of the Lady in Black (1974)
: *aka Il profumo della signora in nero*

Raw (2015)
: *aka Grave*

The Satanic Rites of Dracula (1973)

The Seventh Seal (1957)
: *aka Det sjunde inseglet*

Spirits of the Dead (1968)
: *aka Histoires extraordinaires*

Suspiria (1977)

The Tenant (1976)
: *aka Le locataire*

Them (2006)
: *aka Ils*

Tombs of the Blind Dead (1972)
: *aka La noche del terror ciego*

Vampyr (1932)
: *aka Vampyr – der traum des Allan Gray*

Werewolf Woman (1976)
: *aka La lupa mannara*

The White Reindeer (1952)
: *aka Valkoinen peura*

Who Can Kill A Child? (1976)
: *aka ¿Quién puede matar a un niño?*

Zeder (1983)

Acknowledgements

Thanks must go to Steve J. Shaw, who unhesitatingly agreed to take on a semi-sequel to a book that wasn't even published yet. For background, insights, and general scholarly acumen, I am indebted to Jonathan Rigby and his indispensable book *Euro Gothic*. Although the events recounted in the vignette that opens this book are obviously fictitious, many of the finer details are not, and for those I must acknowledge Tim Lucas and his seminal *Mario Bava: All the Colours of the Dark*. And as always, thanks above all to Lynda E. Rucker for her continual support and encouragement.

One book and sadly several months too late, I would also like to acknowledge the support of the much-missed David Hall, a perfect gentleman who offered some unsolicited and gratefully appreciated assistance upon the completion of *England's Screaming*. There are never enough people like David in the world, and now, tragically, there is one less.

Now available and forthcoming from
Black Shuck Shadows:

blackshuckbooks.co.uk/shadows